"I've
like

His dark eyes smiled down at her as he spoke. Samantha frowned. *The oldest cliché in the book,* she told herself.

And yet...she wanted to believe that he was telling the truth. That she was special to him. She tried to ignore the sly inner voice with its nagging suspicions. "Really?" she asked, her voice falsely bright. "What makes me so different?"

Josh paused for a moment. "You're cranky, irritating, frustrating, maddening..."

"You sure know how to pay a compliment."

"...interesting, sexy, exciting, fascinating." His head bent lower so that his lips were by her ear. "Sam? You know I'm crazy about you, don't you?"

Anger, unhappiness and confusion mixed chaotically in her head. The ship's ballroom seemed to slip and spin about her, but she managed to extricate herself from his arms and shove him away.

She would not be manipulated this way. She would not!

CLAIRE HARRISON works hard at writing—and loves it. After all, she says, hers is one of the few professions that allows one to earn a living, have a choice of heroes and play God with hundreds of characters. Now that her husband, a scientist, is no longer posted in Washington, she and her family make their home in Canada.

Books by Claire Harrison

HARLEQUIN PRESENTS
671—PROPHECY OF DESIRE
705—DANCE WHILE YOU CAN
727—LEADING MAN
736—ONCE A LOVER
753—AN INDEPENDENT WOMAN
760—DRAGON'S POINT
769—ONE LAST DANCE
906—DIPLOMATIC AFFAIR
930—LOVE IS A DISTANT SHORE

CLAIRE HARRISON

fantasy unlimited

Harlequin Books

TORONTO • NEW YORK • LONDON
AMSTERDAM • PARIS • SYDNEY • HAMBURG
STOCKHOLM • ATHENS • TOKYO • MILAN

Harlequin Presents first edition October 1987
ISBN 0-373-11018-9

Original hardcover edition published in 1987
by Mills & Boon Limited

CHAPTER ONE

SAMANTHA LORIMER gazed uneasily at her grandmother, who sat in the chair opposite her. As usual, the old lady stuck out like a sore thumb in the elegant morning room with its carved antiques, its Picassos, its luxury and its general air of money spent without any thought to expense. Margaret was wearing one of her typical outfits, her tiny form clothed in frayed designer jeans and a smock with two missing buttons. On her feet were white socks and an old pair of men's brown leather slippers. Around her forehead was a red, white and blue striped jogger's headband, and her hair had been pulled back into a white and untidy bun. Her only concession to her wealth and position was the double strand of pearls around her neck and the six rings that adorned her paint-stained fingers. Their diamonds, emeralds, rubies and sapphires glittered at Samantha as Margaret poured herself a cup of steaming, fragrant tea.

'Now,' she said, giving Samantha a severe look over her pince-nez glasses, 'it's time to get down to business.'

'Business?' Samantha asked warily.

'Yes, business—you. You're vegetating. If we don't do something you're going to be as petrified as the Petrified Forest. It's got to come to a stop. I refuse to have a granddaughter who's permanently stuck into frump!'

'Grandma, I. . .'

'Margaret. Call me Margaret.'

Samantha had forgotten the recent edict that Margaret had laid down to the family. All grandchildren beyond the age of consent were no longer to call her by that childish epithet. The name 'Grandma', she had proclaimed, when spoken by a grown-up grandchild, sounded ridiculous and made her feel ancient, and if there was one thing that Margaret Lorimer didn't feel, it was her age. She was a tiny, wrinkled woman with a fierce spirit, crackling blue eyes and a face whose former beauty could still be found in her high cheekbones and delicately cleft chin. Margaret, now in her seventieth year, had outlived three husbands and grown more eccentric with each passing decade.

'Margaret,' Samantha said carefully, 'I'm fine. Really.'

Her grandmother gave an unladylike snort. 'I'm neither blind nor senile, young lady.'

'I love my job, my apartment, my. . .'

Another snort. 'Working yourself into an absolute frazzle! That law office hasn't done you an ounce of good. All it's done is keep your nose pressed sharply to the grindstone.'

To Samantha this was familiar ground. She and Margaret had tussled over it before, their separate philosophies crashing head-on. Margaret had never been able to understand the enjoyment Samantha got out of poring through large, dusty tomes and spending long hours in abstract thinking. 'I like practising law,' she said firmly. 'There's nothing else I'd rather do.'

Margaret, as she was apt to do, ignored her. 'And take a good look at you!' Samantha glanced uneasily down at her plaid skirt, crossed knees, stockinged calves and sensible black pumps. 'Prim and proper like some Victorian virgin. Ten pounds overweight. A hairdo that would look good on a eighty-year-old.'

'Ouch!' said Samantha, wincing. In addition to all her other peculiar characteristics, Margaret Lorimer was blunt.

'Well, you're not denying any of it, are you?'

'I'm on a diet, and I have an appointment at the hairdresser's. It's just that I've been too busy to get my hair cut, and I grab food when I can. I do try to exercise, but there's never enough time and. . .'

'And sex? What about that?'

Samantha was halted in her tracks. 'Sex?'

'Hmmph!' Margaret snorted triumphantly. 'I knew it! Barely knows what the word means.'

'Margaret, I. . .'

'. . . and practically non-existent in your case, I'd say. Oh, I know there's been the odd man hanging around. An occasional lover.' Samantha opened her mouth and then closed it; with Margaret, discretion was the better part of valour. 'But that isn't enough. Not for a Lorimer woman.' Margaret leaned forward and gave Samantha a piercing look. 'You need a man, my dear, a red-blooded man. Someone who will remind you that you're a woman.'

'I'd rather not. . .'

The blue eyes above the prince-nez glasses glittered frostily at her. 'Samantha, I won't put up with it any more.'

Samantha blinked. 'With what?'

'With you and the way you treat yourself.' She put up a gnarled hand to stop Samantha's objections. 'I've made my decision.'

'Grand. . . Margaret, except for the ten pounds, I'm happy the way I am.'

'Hmmph!'

'I have a very full and very satisfying life.'

'Is there a man in it?'

'Well, not exactly, but. . .'

'Hmmmph!' And this 'hmmmph' was accompanied with action. Margaret stood up, grabbed Samantha by the elbow so that she was forced to stand as well, then marched her over to the full-length mirror in the hallway. 'There,' she added triumphantly, 'what do you see?'

Samantha stared and tried to see herself through her grandmother's eyes. What she saw was a woman, dressed like all the other women lawyers in her office, in a blazer, blouse and skirt, an outfit that was conservative and concealing. She had an oval face, a delicate nose and lips that curved into a small smile, putting a dimple in each cheek. Her hair was a rich dark brown, shoulder-length, parted in the middle and pulled back on each side behind ears which were small and adorned with tiny pearl earrings. Her eyes were wide and blue but hidden by gold-rimmed glasses. There was, Samantha saw, nothing special about the woman in the mirror. She was average in every respect; average in height, in weight, and in looks.

'Well,' she said hesitantly, 'it looks like me.'

Her grandmother's reflection glared at her. 'That, my dear, is the problem we have to face.'

'It is?'

'There is no reason why you have to look like a woman lawyer who needs a jazzy wardrobe, or up-to-date haircut, a diet and a good healthy dose of hanky-panky.'

'Grandma!'

'Margaret, and don't interrupt me now. Cassie!'

Cassie arrived in the hallway, grinning from ear to ear and bearing two large manila envelopes in her hands. She was the same age as Margaret, a tall angular woman who had kept her Irish brogue although she had left Dublin for New York half a century ago.

'Is the lass ready?' she asked Margaret.

'She'll never be ready, Cassie,' Margaret said severely. 'This isn't one of those things I could lead her into gently. We're going to have to push her full speed ahead, spoon-feed her, so to speak.'

'Now, Margaret,' Samantha began, 'what on earth are you talking about?'

But Margaret refused to answer and beckoned Samantha to follow her back into the morning room.

'All right,' she said as they sat back down in the winged chairs. 'Envelope number one.'

Cassie handed a thick envelope to Samantha with a wide smile. 'It'd do ye a world of good,' she said.

Samantha turned the envelope over in her hand and gave it a distrustful glance. It had nothing written on it except her name in large block letters. She looked at her grandmother. 'What is it?' she asked.

'Open it, and you'll find out.' Margaret was also smiling and sitting on the edge of her chair.

'Will it explode?' Samantha asked teasingly.

'Open it, you obstinate child!'

Samantha tore open the end of the envelope, turned it upside down and let a mass of papers and brochures tumble out. Glossy pictures of rocky islands set against the turquoise backdrop of the Mediterranean Sea lay in her lap. A PanAm ticket lay on top of a cheque for several thousands of dollars. A neatly typed itinerary had fallen to her feet.

She gave Margaret a look of surprise. 'It's. . . it's a trip,' she said at last.

'Not just a trip,' Margaret said smugly. 'A vacation. Three days in Athens and a two-week cruise through the Greek Islands on the *Princess Marguerita*. There can't be anything wrong with a ship with a name like that, eh, Cassie?'

'Heavens, no. She'll be a honey of a ship.'

'Plus a little spending money and, if you look a bit deeper, you'll find a Miracle Morning at Elizabeth Arden's and a membership of a health club uptown. I don't want you going away on a trip ten pounds overweight with your hair looking like something the dog dragged in.'

'Margaret, I don't believe. . . why, this is. . .'

'And,' said Margaret with a final flourish, 'I've arranged for you to see my optometrist. Those glasses of yours have got to go. I want you to get contact lenses.'

Samantha smiled at her grandmother and decided not to tell her that she'd never been able to tolerate contact lenses. She simply leaned forward and kissed Margaret's wrinkled cheek. 'It's wonderful,' she said. 'Truly wonderful.'

Margaret beamed; Cassie beamed.

'But I. . . I can't go.'

The beams ceased and were replaced by frowns.

'Are ye crazy?' Cassie asked.

'Why not?' demanded Margaret.

'Because I have such a heavy work schedule and there's a trial coming up in a month just when you've scheduled the trip and. . .'

'Nonsense,' Margaret said with sniff. 'Horsefeathers.'

'But I really appreciate it. I love the idea. It's a wonderful, thoughtful and. . .'

'I called your office, spoke to your boss—a dear man, by the way—and arranged for you to have a holiday.'

Samantha sat back. 'You did *what*? How did you ever. . .?' She was trying to imagine her gruff and quick-tempered boss, Tom, as a 'dear man'.

'I practised the Lorimer charm on him,' Margaret explained with satisfaction, 'and told him that his law firm was driving you into an early grave. Samantha, my dear, according to his records you haven't taken a vacation in over a year and a half. He quite agreed with me that you were as stale as a doughnut left out overnight.'

Samantha couldn't help wincing at the idea of Tom and Margaret having a cosy discussion over her physical and mental state, but she did have to acknowledge the fact that she was tired, run-down and in desperate need of some rest and relaxation.

'So ye'll go?' asked Cassie.

Samantha looked up into her worried, angular face, realised how much this gift meant to both of them, and knew she couldn't refuse. 'Of course,' she said. 'I don't think I can resist.'

'Good,' said Margaret. 'Cassie, envelope number two.'

'You mean there's more?' Samantha asked as she took the second envelope.

'This is the best part,' said Margaret, and Samantha could see that this was true. The gift of a cruise, spending money, hairdresser, contact lenses and membership of a health spa was nothing compared to what was coming up. Both Margaret and Cassie had lit up like two overcharged light bulbs.

The envelope was thin and, when Samantha opened it, only one piece of paper fell into her hands.

She gingerly unfolded it and then stared at its brief message. The letterhead had one name on it, 'Fantasy Unlimited', and a small black and white logo of a plump, grinning genie rubbing a tiny Aladdin's lamp. Below that was a single sentence: 'In compliance with your own private fantasy, a shipboard romance in the Greek Islands.'

Samantha read it once, read it again, then stared at it with disbelieving eyes. Finally she looked up to meet Margaret's avid gaze. 'What in God's name is this?'

'Just what it says,' Margaret said gleefully.

'A shipboard romance?' Samantha glanced back at the paper. 'Your own private fantasy. Did you,' she said to Margaret in slow and carefully enunciated words, 'pay this. . . this company, Fantasy Unlimited, for me to have a shipboard romance on my cruise to the Greek Islands?'

'Isn't it a marvellous gift?'

'With some paid gigolo!'

'Now, hold your horses. It's an escort service. You know, a handsome man will be at your side, join you for dinner, dance with you under the moonlight—that sort of thing.'

'That sort of thing,' Samantha echoed coldly.

'And if that sort of thing turns into another sort of thing. . . well,' Margaret gave an eloquent shrug, 'who's to know?'

'Do you think I'd go to bed with a man who's been paid to provide me with a. . . a. . .' Samantha was stammering now with a suppressed fury, 'a stud service?'

It was Margaret's turn to wince and she looked at Cassie. 'Definitely stuffy,' she commented.

'No one's forcing ye into anything, lass. We just wanted you to have a wee bit of fun.'

'And I'm fully capable of finding my own men, thank you!'

'We know you are, dear,' Margaret said soothingly, 'but we just thought we'd help nature along.'

Samantha stood up. 'I won't go,' she said. 'Thank you for everything, but I absolutely will not go if some man is going to be hanging around me earning his living by pretending to find me romantic and attractive.'

Margaret sighed. 'All right,' she said.

But Samantha was still infuriated and didn't catch her grandmother's words. 'I can't imagine anything more insulting, more demeaning, more disgusting than paying a man to make love to me! It's horrible, that's what it is, and. . .'

Margaret had stood up and taken Samantha's hands. 'Sam dear, it's all right. I'll cancel Fantasy Unlimited.'

Samantha blinked and looked down at her. 'You will?'

'Of course. I don't want you to be unhappy, and I think you should take the trip.'

'You promise that you'll cancel?'

'Cross my heart.' And Margaret dramatically crossed her forearms over her tiny, meagre chest.

Samantha gave her a suspicious glance. 'I don't know,' she said. 'You're not the world's most trustworthy person.'

Cassie intervened, 'Don't worry your head about it. I'll make sure that she cancels.'

Samantha glanced at Cassie. Where Margaret was flighty, eccentric and disorganised, Cassie was reliable, pragmatic and sensible. Margaret's promises were as ephemeral as the air: Cassie's words were as solid as the rock of Gibraltar. 'All right,' she said. 'I'll go.'

'Good,' said Margaret with relief.

'But,' Samantha added, shaking a finger at her, 'no more funny business!'

Margaret gave her a reproachful look. 'Of course not!'

'Okay,' Samantha agreed, 'but the two of you should be ashamed of yourselves. Really! What would people think if I told them that my grandmother had tried to buy me a lover?'

'They'd think you were lucky,' Margaret said tartly. 'It's better than what most grandmothers give their grandaughters. Toaster ovens, ironing boards, knitted scarves, underpants.' Her already wrinkled face creased in disgust and she added with hauteur, 'At least I have some imagination!'

Joshua Baxter Sinclair was sitting in front of the desk in his well-appointed office and staring down at the three files in front of him. One had to do with the acquisition of an office building on Lexington Avenue, another reflected the massive amounts of work already done about the purchase of a condominium complex in New Jersey, and the third one had his own name on it. This latter file had been pulled by his secretary and dropped on his desk with a brief and unrevealing memo attached to it that said, 'Brought to your attention at the request of your partners.'

Josh stared at it, opened it and idly sifted through the papers inside. There were Internal Revenue Service forms, deduction slips, stock certificates and bonus announcements. It was the sort of personal file that demonstrated in a cold and efficient fashion that J.B. Sinclair was a partner in Drexel, Ross, Beame and Sinclair Associates, that he'd been in the partnership for eight years, that he was thirty-nine years old and that he had no dependants. It also showed that since his arrival in the partnership, his annual income had quadrupled and was a combination of salary, commissions, stock options and bonuses. And, while none of the papers actually had anything to say about J.B. Sinclair's personality or temperament, it would have been clear to anyone reading it that to survive in the jungle that was Manhattan's real estate business, he was shrewd, patient, aggressive and hard-working. All in all, it was a very satisfactory file, and Josh couldn't imagine why his partners had had it sent to him this particular morning.

Shaking his head in bewilderment, he turned to the two other files and immersed himself in them. He had a rough day ahead. There were meetings with three clients, two of whom were close to a major real estate agreement. He had a lunch date with a local politican who was in the powerful position of presiding over City Hall's committee on property re-evaluation and, because he was the one of the four partners considered to possess the most tact and charm, he'd been assigned the difficult task of meeting that evening with a Saudi Arabian prince who was looking into Manhattan real estate. It was a harder day than he usually had because it had begun at six in the morning when he'd got up and jogged, and it would continue on to all hours of the night, if rumours about the Prince were true. But Josh was used to working hard. An eighty-hour week was nothing new.

He worked at the files until ten-thirty when his secretary put her head round the door and told him that coffee was arriving along with Bud Drexel. Josh stood up from his black leather chair, stretched a bit and walked over to the window where he looked down

thirty storeys to the street below. Against the backdrop of the Manhattan skyline, he was a tall figure,
broad-shouldered in his grey suit and dark-haired.
He had a handsome face with deep-set brown eyes,
a square chin, a wide forehead. It was the sort of face
that looked lived-in; the kind that showed the imprint
of many emotions. There were deep brackets by a
mouth that could set itself at a severe angle when its
owner was angry or upset. Yet it was also a mouth
that could curve into a long, slow and lazy smile, the
kind of smile that made women's heads turn and their
hearts melt.

'Well, Josh, how goes it?'

He turned to face Bud Drexel, who stood in the
doorway. They were partners in business and close
friends. Josh had known Bud since college days.
They'd gone their separate ways after graduation.
Josh had got a degree in business administration and
had worked in banking for five years. Bud had gone
to work for his father, a man who already had his finger in numerous business and real estate deals in the
city. When Bud Drexel Senior had died, Bud had
expanded his one-man operation to three and then
asked Josh to join in. It had been a profitable merger
for all of them.

'Not bad,' he said. 'Could be worse.' There was no
particular use in elaborating further on his day. Bud
knew precisely what Josh was up to and vice versa.
Business arrangements for the week were always discussed at a partnership meeting that was held every
Monday morning at eight-thirty sharp.

Bud sat down on the leather couch, and its frame
creaked beneath his weight.

'Carol,' he said idly, 'tells me that we haven't seen
you in weeks.'

Josh gave him a curious glance and sat back down in the chair behind his wide mahogany desk. During the working day, the partners of Drexel, Ross, Beame and Sinclair Associates talked about business, the stock and bond market, the latest football scores and politics. They didn't discuss their private or social lives. By unspoken agreement, such topics were discussed after work over cocktails or by telephoning a partner's home.

'No,' he agreed, 'it's been a while.'

'Hell, Josh,' protested Bud, 'it isn't like you need a formal invitation, is it? You're welcome at our place any time.'

'I know that,' Josh said with a smile. Carol, Bud and their two children had been his home away from home whenever he felt the need for a relaxed domesticity and a warm family setting.

'So? When will you grace our house with your presence?'

'Any time.'

'Saturday?'

'Sure.'

'For dinner?'

'No problem.'

'You want to bring anyone?' Bud asked nonchalantly.

Josh shook his head. 'Nope. I'm a lone wolf now.'

'I see.'

There was a short and tactful silence as Bud forbore from mentioning the last lady who had occupied Josh's leisure time and intimate moments. She had been notable for her beauty, her style of dressing, her high spirits and her social connections. But she'd possessed, as far as Bud was concerned, an alarming lack of loyalty.

Bud shifted uncomfortably in his seat and changed the subject. 'Hey,' he said, 'Drexel, Ross and Beame have a surprise for you.'

'A surprise?'

'Did you look through your personal file?'

'Well, I glanced through it,' said Josh, then added jokingly, 'I wondered if my resignation notice was in there.'

'Nope. You're still on the payroll.'

Josh took the file out of his Out basket and stared at it. 'What am I supposed to find in here?'

Bud grinned and stared up at the ceiling. 'We noticed something in that file.'

'What?'

'That you haven't taken a vacation since last year.'

'I went skiing last winter.'

'That was for the Thanksgiving weekend,' Bud retorted. 'I'm talking about a month-long, let-it-all-hang-out, relax-in-the-sun holiday. You know, wine, women, song.'

'Bud, you know I. . .' Josh paused, and a certain grimness settled in around his mouth.

'I know that ever since you broke up with Nadja, you've been working too hard. I find you here in the morning when I come and you're here at night when I leave. I've even heard from the janitor that you're here at the weekends. I understood it at first, but it's enough, Josh. You're going to drive yourself right into a heart attack!'

'You don't understand. . .'

'The hell I don't!' Bud sat forward, his round face earnest and concerned. 'She played with you, that's what she did. She had her fun fooling around and then she took off for greener pastures. Look, she was beautiful enough to drive any man around the bend,

I'll grant you that, but she isn't worth a second's thought—she never was.'

Josh tried to get a word in edgeways, but Bud was going full steam ahead.

'Carol saw it coming, she really did. "Bud," she'd say, "that woman's going to hurt Josh. She wants more than he'll ever be able to give her." She came from too much money and she wanted more—that's the way I saw it. She thought she was a damned princess and you were a commoner.'

Bud took a breath and Josh said quickly, 'It's over, Bud. I accepted that months ago.' And he had, but what he hadn't been able to overcome was the residue of bitterness that was left.

'Well then,' said Bud, his face lighting up, 'there's no reason why you won't use the tickets in the file, is there?'

'What tickets?'

'The ones for the trip to Greece and the cruise around the Greek Islands.'

Josh opened the file again, flipped through the papers and found the tickets. 'Welcome to the *Princess Marguerita*—Your Floating Resort.' He held up the envelope and stared at Bud. 'What the hell is this?'

'I told you—it's a vacation. We've booked you up for two weeks; we figured that you'd find something to do for the other two.'

'You did this? And John? And Peter?'

'You don't think that three guys who can put together a multi-million-dollar deal involving three countries and five currencies can't manage one short holiday?'

'This is very kind of you, but. . .'

'But what?'

'But I've got so much work. . .'

'The hell with the work. We'll fill in for you.'

'And I couldn't. . .' Josh's voice trailed off, How could he say that nothing in life excited him any more, that he had got so damned cynical about happiness that he never expected to find it again?

Bud leaned forward, his voice quiet but insistent. 'Go, Josh. You need the rest. You're going to work yourself into a nervous breakdown. We all know it—we've been watching you.'

Josh took a deep breath and glanced at the tickets. He was tired, he admitted that, more tired than he'd ever been in his life. He was weary from hours of work, from a lonely apartment and a bitter heart. He hated the idea of travelling by himself, but he was touched by the effort his partners had made. Who was he to take away from them the pleasures of generosity?

'Okay,' he said. 'You win.'

Bud grinned from ear to ear. 'Great!' And he leaned forward and pressed the buzzer on Josh's desk.

There was a sudden flurry in his doorway as John Beame and Peter Ross appeared. They were carrying champagne and four champagne goblets. Josh stared at them as the bottle was uncorked and each glass was filled with bubbly. 'Isn't this going a little too far?' he asked.

No one listened to him.

'To Josh's holiday,' said Peter. 'May he sunburn all to hell.'

'To his cruise,' John said. 'May he come back an expert on Greece.'

'To his time off,' said Bud. 'May he meet a lovely and willing lady.'

Josh couldn't help grinning. 'Listen, you sadists, you know who you meet on these cruises? Lonely, middle-aged women. I've heard all about them. All they want to do is find a man.'

'I'll drink to that,' Peter said, and they all lifted their glasses.

CHAPTER TWO

IT WAS hard not to feel like royalty, Samantha thought with an inward sigh, as the steward in his crisp white uniform led her down to the C deck of the *Princess Marguerita* and smartly opened the door to her stateroom. From the time that she'd arrived on the boat she'd been treated with smiles, friendliness and courtesy. The purser had welcomed her like an old friend; the steward had assured her that she had one of the nicest staterooms on the boat. Everything had been so organised and efficient that she was already starting to feel slightly better after what had turned out to be a hair-raising, turbulent flight to Athens, a gruelling wait through Greek Customs and an unnerving taxi ride to the docks.

After tipping the steward and seeing him out of the door, she sighed thankfully, kicked off her shoes and sank into one of the chairs. Margaret's propensity for going first-class, she decided, suited her to a T. The carpet under her stockinged toes was a plush pale blue, the chair was a darker blue velvet and, on the white lacquered table beside her, was a vase of fresh flowers and an attractive fruit basket wrapped in cellophane.

Across from her, hanging on the wall, was a mirror, and as she stared into it, Samantha also had to concede that Margaret's energy, money and insistence on value had wrought another miracle. Even without a night's sleep, an over-exposure to Athens'

tropical temperature and a smashing headache,
Samantha still looked as if she'd come out of a bandbox. Not that it hadn't taken effort. For a month
before the cruise, she had given her body and soul
over to an assortment of specialists—exercise
instructors, hairdressers, diet consultants, cosmetic
specialists and sales clerks. She'd had facials, pedi-
cures, body massages and manicures. She'd been
weighed, measured, pummelled, talked at and
organised. She'd managed to lose twelve pounds, find
an entirely new wardrobe and, surprise of surprises,
be fitted with the latest in contact lenses, the kind that
she could wear comfortably night and day for two or
three weeks at a time without taking them out.

The result was a new Samantha that the old one
was still trying to get used to. Her hair had been cut
so that it formed a dark cap around her head and then
waved so that it curled defiantly despite wind or rain
or humidity. She'd learned to apply cosmetics that
emphasised the high cheekbones in her now slender
face, tilted her eyes into thick dark lashes and out-
lined the softness of her lips. And she was now dressed
in clothes whose bright colours dimmed the memory
of her dark, conservative business suits. She had a
suitcase full of sundresses with low-cut backs, light-
weight slacks and sheer tops.

Margaret had approved of everything, then pursed
her lips in calculation and announced that Samantha
wasn't quite finished yet. Ignoring all protests, she
had called a taxi and dragged Samantha to a lingerie
shop, where she had gone through the racks and
boxes like some miniature whirlwind. Samantha had
watched with alarm as the pile of froth and silk grew
on the store's counter. It included bras made of wisps
of lace, panties cut so high on the sides that, when

she'd tried them on, her thighs had developed vertigo, and a scandalous see-through nightie that left so little to the imagination that she had wondered out loud what its use was.

'It's the last curtain to rise before the play begins, my dear,' Margaret had said dreamily. 'That last tantalising obstacle.'

'You told me you'd cancel that Fantasy Unlimited contract,' Samantha said suspiciously.

'I did, but that's no reason to give up hope.'

'I'm going on a cruise, not an orgy!'

'The two,' Margaret had said tartly, 'are not necessarily diametrically opposed to one another.'

So here she was, at last, in her luxurious and well-appointed stateroom, ready for the great adventure, whatever that would turn out to be. Well, not quite ready. Being a tidy person, Samantha wanted to unpack and put her clothes away. And there was still a shower to take and a nap to enjoy on that lovely gold bedspread that she could see through the open door of her bedroom. She raised her arms and stretched them over her head in a graceful gesture and then, with a contented sigh, got up and headed towards the tiny bathroom.

'Room 1510. Here we are, sir—a double with a sitting room. I hope you'll find it to your taste.'

'I'm sure I will.'

'There's a small bar here behind the panelling.'

'Very nice.'

'Closet space and. . .'

'That's fine. I'll show myself around.'

'Of course, sir.'

'Thanks very much.'

'Thank you, sir.' And, with a generous tip in hand, the steward scurried away.

Josh sighed, pushed his two leather suitcases to one side, and decided to pour himself a drink first thing. He was supposed to be relaxed and here he was, strung up as tight as a rubber band. Well, he was only one day away from the office and all its headaches. That last deal before he had left had been the straw that broke the camel's back, and he'd been willing to admit, without shame, that if he didn't take a break from meetings and agendas and long-distance phone calls, he'd collapse. He rubbed the back of his neck with a weary hand and then pulled open the panelling, revealing a row of small bottles, several glasses and a small refrigerator which, on inspection, housed a very adequate supply of ice and chilled mixes.

The first sip of Scotch burned its way down, but the second swallow warmed him with that internal amber glow. He sighed again, looked around him and admired the décor of the room, the attractive blues and whites, the comfortable-looking couch, the fruit and cheese basket on the table. He was hungry, he realised. There had been too many hours since he'd eaten that abominable creation the airline called lunch. Josh sat down, tore the cellophane off the fruit basket and picked out a small packet of Gouda. For a few minutes, he sipped at his Scotch, nibbled at his cheese and let the tension drain out of him.

Then he stood up, unbuttoned his shirt, stretched luxuriously and ran a hand across the broad expanse of his chest. It was a man's gesture of contentment, reflecting Josh's sudden realisation that he had a month ahead of him that would be well and truly free from the pressures of clients and partners. No more suits and ties, no more velvet-glove treatments of prickly Arab magnates, no more wrangles with bureaucrats at City Hall whose knowledge of the building code was less than his. From here on out it was jeans and sweats, hours in the warm Greek sun and the freedom to do and say what he pleased.

Another long swallow of Scotch made him feel even more mellow. He glanced around the stateroom and decided to investigate his new home, starting with the bedroom. After all, he thought with a touch of amused cynicism, wasn't that where his partners intended his 'fun' to take place? According to them he was supposed to lure willing and nubile young women into his stateroom and partake of the pleasures of the flesh. Well, he couldn't care less.

He turned the knob and pushed open the door to his bedroom. He was so buried in his thoughts that for a moment he didn't notice what was wrong with the room. Then, when he did, he stared for a few seconds, because he couldn't believe what he did see. Finally, he walked over to the bed and looked down at the woman lying there, in a sleep so deep that not even the sound of him entering the room had caused her to move.

She lay on her back, one bare arm flung up over her head. Dark curls tumbled against the pillow and dark lashes lay in small crescents on a face that was slender and fine-boned. Her lips were pink, slightly parted and curved upwards as if she were enjoying a pleasant dream. The sheet had slipped down to her waist, revealing a delicate gold chain necklace around her neck and firm breasts barely held in by cups of white lace. Through the fabric, her nipples were dusky circles. In the dim, curtained light, her skin was the colour of honey and, for a moment, Josh forgot the past and imagined touching it, reverently, feeling its sleekness and warmth beneath his finger.

Then the woman moved, and he remembered.

'What the hell are you doing here?'

The words, spoken in a deep, masculine growl, made Samantha slowly lift the heaviness that was her eyelids.

The first two things she noticed about the face she was staring into were that it was exceedingly handsome and very angry. The two facts did not eliminate one another. Anger made the dark eyes narrow seductively beneath the dark brows and caused the mouth to twist into a sexy slant. Then she noticed that the face was attached, via the neck of course, to a chest bared by the flaring edges of his white shirt. It was the kind of chest that was covered with a wide triangle of hair that ended in a dark line running down into a belted pair of grey slacks. The attractiveness of that chest enhanced rather than detracted from the face glaring down at her.

What a lovely man, Samantha thought with the lazy thoughts of someone who has just come awake and not quite realised when or where she was. What a lovely, sexy man.

'And I will repeat myself,' said the voice. 'What the hell are you doing here?'

Samantha's eyes snapped open. She blinked and the room came into sharp focus. Her mistake was suddenly glaringly obvious. What she had thought was a sexy apparition had turned into an irate man with a half-opened shirt and a drink in his hand.

'I beg your pardon?' she struggled to sit up, suddenly recalled her near nudity and, in a panic, pulled the sheet up to her neck so that all that appeared of her was a shocked expression, wide blue eyes and a dishevelled head of dark curls.

'What are you doing in my room?'

'I could,' she said, clearing her throat, 'ask you the same question.'

'You happen to be in my bed.'

'I am not!'

'Look, Miss Whoever-You-Are, this is my state-room, my bedroom and, without a doubt, my bed. And I have not invited you to share it.'

'Now just a minute,' Samantha said hotly. 'I don't have to ask anyone to share what is legally mine.'

The voice was cold. 'You deny that you're in the wrong room?'

She lifted her chin. 'Absolutely.'

'Just a minute. I'll be right back.'

The stranger turned and left, revealing as he went that he was the possessor of broad shoulders, a straight back, lean hips, long legs and a stride that spoke, Samantha noted dismally, of utter conviction.

While he was gone, she grabbed her white terry-cloth bathrobe from the chair beside the bed, but didn't have enough time to put it on before he was back, waving a slip of paper in the air. She hurriedly pulled the sheet back up to her chin.

'Room 1510,' he said smugly. 'That's what it says here. Joshua Baxter Sinclair, Room 1510.'

Samantha aimed for dignity and her best legal manner. 'And you are, I presume, Mr Sinclair.'

'None other.'

'Well, I have a similar slip of paper, Mr Sinclair.'

'Really?'

'Really,' she said icily.

But she saw that he was sure of his position now. In fact, he was in the act of making himself right at home in her bedroom. He had put down the drink he'd been carrying on her bedside table and now sat himself down on the chair that had been previously occupied by her bathrobe.

'And where would that be?'

'In. . .' Oh, hell, where had she put that slip of paper that the purser had given her? She was generally so neat that she kept everything she owned in its right and proper place. Unfortunately, for the life of her, she couldn't now remember where she had put that damned slip of paper.

'In your bag?' he said caustically, taking a sip of Scotch.

'No.' She would have remembered that, remembered opening the clasp and sticking the paper in. She frantically scoured her memory, knowing full well that she, Samantha Lorimer, lawyer and Phi Beta Kappa, was coming across like the world's scattiest female.

'Your suitcase,' he said with a show of barely disguised impatience.

'No. . .' And then it all came back to her with a rush of relief. 'It's in the pocket of my skirt.'

'Very good,' he said as if she were a small and wayward child, and Samantha couldn't help wincing. 'Miss. . . what is your name anyway?'

'Lorimer. Samantha Lorimer.'

'All right, Miss Lorimer, why don't you get your room number assignment out of the pocket of your skirt and we'll examine it to see where you made your mistake.'

God, but she hated patronising men! 'The steward brought me to this room, Mr Sinclair,' she pointed out in precise tones.

'All right—where the steward made his mistake.' There was a long silence while he took another sip of his Scotch and then, looking at her again, he said, 'Well?'

'I can hardly,' said Samantha, 'get out of bed with you sitting there.'

'Oh?' he asked infuriatingly.

'I am not dressed, Mr Sinclair.'

'I have already noted, Miss Lorimer, that you wear a Bali bra with underwires and a front hook.'

Samantha couldn't help it—she blushed, deeply and profoundly, and she hated blushing. She was thirty years old and far too mature to be caught with an adolescent stain of pink on her cheeks. Her embarrassment caused her tone of voice to be sharper than it might have been otherwise. 'You're very observant, Mr Sinclair.'

He nodded, accepting the words as a compliment rather than the sarcasm they were meant to be. 'I've been told that before.'

By this time, Samantha's embarrassment and irritation had turned into fury. 'I'm really not interested in your past achievements,' she said through clenched teeth. 'Would you please get out of this room while I dress?'

Damn him, but he was grinning now. 'As long as you don't dawdle.'

Samantha's jaw felt as if it had set into permanent clenched rigidity. 'I never dawdle,' she said, drawing herself up with hauteur and losing the protective shield of her sheet in the process.

Joshua Baxter Sinclair leaned over, plucked the sheet up with his fingers, neatly twisted its hem into a little knot and deftly inserted it in the front of her bra. 'Style number 1620,' he said. 'Size 34B.'

Samantha's voice deserted her, emerging out of her throat as an incoherent, gargling sound, so it wasn't until the door was shut behind him that she managed to get the words out.

'34C, you bastard!' she yelled.

The door swung open and Josh stuck his head in. 'Sorry,' he said with a grin, then shut the door again.

It took Samantha ten minutes to get dressed, brush her teeth and reassemble the bits and pieces of her shredded dignity. In all her intimate dealings with men, which admittedly had not been great in number or long in duration, she had never found herself in the position she'd been in with Joshua Sinclair. And, while its intimacy was only accidental, nevertheless, she couldn't remember a time when she'd felt so vulnerable, so exposed or so humiliated. Samantha was used to being in control. Now she had discovered that someone else could have the upper hand and refuse to yield it no matter how cool and aloof she became. Not only was this a new experience, but she also didn't like it. Not at all.

Well, thank heavens the ship was large enough so that, when the room problem did sort itself out, she would be able to avoid the obnoxious Mr Sinclair without any difficulty. She would make sure that they had different dinner seatings to begin with and, since the boat had duplicates of almost everything—bars, lounges, swimming pools, games areas—she wouldn't feel at all put out if she had to leave because he was already in it. Furthermore, if they happened to bump into one another on a staircase or in a narrow corridor—well, she'd just give him a cold smile and walk on with her head up high to show him that she didn't give a damn that he'd happened to come upon her sleeping and half-naked.

Samantha couldn't help squirming whenever that thought came to her. It wasn't as if she were a teenager or a hysterical virgin, but still there was something so. . . so awful about having a strange man watching her when she was unconscious, with his eyes able to roam wherever they wished and rest on whatever pleased them. And, of course, she knew exactly what had taken Joshua Sinclair's interest, didn't she? Underwires, indeed! And, for a second, just before she went out into the sitting room where he was no doubt enjoying another drink and the memory of what he'd just put her through, Samantha was consumed with curiosity about a man who knew so much about women's underwear that he recognised brand names and styles. But then she thrust the curiosity away. What did she care anyway?

By the time she entered the sitting room, she had regained her composure, got her unruly curls into submission and looked as cool as a cucumber in a slender white shift and matching white sandals. She found Josh lying down on the couch, his eyes closed, his arms crossed over his still-open shirt. It was her turn to watch him and she took a perverse pleasure in the act, noting the nick beneath his jaw where he'd cut himself shaving and the threads of silver in the dark hair waving over his temples. He was, by anyone's standards, an exceedingly handsome man, but Samantha was determined to find imperfections in that good-looking face.

'Finished looking?' asked Josh, without opening his eyes.

She gritted her teeth. 'I wasn't.'

'You deny it?'

'Absolutely. You don't interest me in the least.'

His eyes flicked open. 'I'd call this a classic case of incompatibility, wouldn't you? We wouldn't have a

1. How do you rate: _____

   (Please print book TITLE)

   1.6 ☐ excellent   .4 ☐ good   .2 ☐ not so good
   .5 ☐ very good   .3 ☐ fair   .1 ☐ poor

2. How likely are you to purchase another book:

   in this *series*?

   2.1 ☐ definitely would purchase
   .2 ☐ probably would purchase
   .3 ☐ probably would not purchase
   .4 ☐ definitely would not purchase

   by this *author*?

   3.1 ☐ definitely would purchase
   .2 ☐ probably would purchase
   .3 ☐ probably would not purchase
   .4 ☐ definitely would not purchase

3. How does this book compare with romance books you usually read?

   4.1 ☐ far better than others
   .2 ☐ better than others
   .3 ☐ about the same
   .4 ☐ not as good
   .5 ☐ definitely not as good

4. Please check the statements you feel best describe this book.

   5 ☐ Realistic conflict
   6 ☐ Too much violence/anger
   7 ☐ Not enough drama
   8 ☐ Especially romantic
   9 ☐ Original plot
   10 ☐ Good humor in story
   11 ☐ Not enough humor
   12 ☐ Not enough description of setting
   13 ☐ Didn't like the subject
   14 ☐ Fast paced
   15 ☐ Too predictable
   16 ☐ Heroine too juvenile/weak/silly
   17 ☐ Believable characters
   18 ☐ Too many foreign/unfamiliar words
   19 ☐ Couldn't put the book down
   20 ☐ Liked the setting
   21 ☐ Made me feel good
   22 ☐ Heroine too independent
   23 ☐ Hero too dominating
   24 ☐ Unrealistic conflict
   25 ☐ Not enough romance
   26 ☐ Too much description of setting
   27 ☐ Ideal hero
   28 ☐ Slow moving
   29 ☐ Not enough suspense
   30 ☐ Liked the subject

5. What aspect of the story outline on the back of the cover appealed to you most?

   31 ☐ location
   33 ☐ characters
   35 ☐ description of conflict
   32 ☐ subject
   34 ☐ element of suspense in plot

6. Did you feel this story was:

   36.1 ☐ too sexy
   .2 ☐ just sexy enough
   .3 ☐ not too sexy

7. Please indicate how many romance paperbacks you read in a month.

   37.1 ☐ 1 to 4   .2 ☐ 5 to 10   .3 ☐ 11 to 15   .4 ☐ more than 15

8. Please indicate your sex and age group.

   38.1 ☐ Male   39.1 ☐ under 18   .3 ☐ 25-34   .5 ☐ 50-64
   .2 ☐ Female   .2 ☐ 18-24   .4 ☐ 35-49   .6 ☐ 65 or older

9. Have you any additional comments about this book?

   (40)_____
   (41)_____
   (42)_____
   (43)_____
   _____
   _____

MABCDEFG

Thank you for completing and returning this questionnaire.

PRINTED IN U.S.A.

NAME _____
(Please Print)

ADDRESS _____

CITY _____

ZIP CODE _____

BUSINESS REPLY MAIL
FIRST CLASS   PERMIT NO. 717   BUFFALO, NY

POSTAGE WILL BE PAID BY ADDRESSEE

NATIONAL READER SURVEYS

901 Fuhrmann Blvd.
P.O. Box 1395
Buffalo, N.Y. 14240-9961

chance of making it as room-mates.'

'We aren't going to *be* room-mates,' Samantha retorted, then waved her slip of paper in the air. 'I have room 1510, too, so the purser obviously made a mistake. I'm sure he'll find some way of fixing it.'

'No doubt.'

But Josh made no effort to get up from the couch. He simply yawned a bit and then closed his eyes again. Samantha stood there for one uncertain minute, then marched up to the couch.

'Well?' she demanded. 'Are we going or not?'

He didn't even have the decency to open his eyes. 'Going where?'

She would have liked to stamp her foot, but she'd given up that habit when she was five years old. 'To the purser's office, of course.'

Josh signed, opened his eyes, reluctantly pulled himself upright and ran his hands through his thick dark hair. 'My dear Miss Lorimer,' he said, 'please sit down.'

'I. . .' But Samantha could see that it wouldn't be of any use to protest, so she unwillingly sat down on the chair beside the couch.

He was appraising her now, his dark eyes amused. 'You match the décor—white and blue.'

'I'm not here to talk about. . .'

'All right,' he said wearily, 'we're going to have to solve the problem of the room, but we'd be crazy to think we could do it now. There's too much confusion, what with the passengers getting on and all the stewards working double time to get everyone sorted out. I suggest waiting an hour or so until things quiet down.'

Samantha didn't want to agree with him, but the argument made sense. She could hear doors slamming outside their room and could imagine the narrow corridors jammed with baggage and passengers and scurrying crew.

'. . , and besides,' Josh went on, 'this is my holiday and I'm damned if I'm going to rush around. Everything will sort itself out eventually.'

Well, she was on vacation, too, and she didn't intend to spend even one minute of it with Joshua Sinclair. She stood up. 'Fine,' she said. 'I'll meet you in the purser's office in an hour.'

Josh eyed her, his glance resting on the curve her breasts made under the light cotton shift. 'Can't stand my company?' he asked with amusement.

She drew herself up. 'Frankly, no.'

'Well,' he said with another yawn as he went back to a prone position on the couch, 'we didn't really start off on the right foot.'

That, Samantha thought as she walked towards the door, was the understatement of the year. Talk about disastrous! Margaret, of course, would have acted in a totally different manner when confronted with a man in what was supposed to be her bedroom. She would have batted her eyelashes, given him a winsome glance and convinced him that there was nothing he wanted more than to find her in his bed. Then the two of them would have ended up in it together.

'You blew it,' Samantha could imagine her grandmother saying. 'Here's a man with looks so good that he should be declared illegal and he doesn't give a damn if he never sees you again.'

'He's obnoxious and insufferable!'

'Tsk-tsk, you've only known him for five minutes. Isn't that jumping to conclusions? And weren't you pretty obnoxious, too?'

Well, she had been and probably still was, but she wasn't going to back down on this one, she thought as she grabbed the knob of the door. She didn't like Joshua Sinclair, no matter how attractive he was. She wouldn't like him if he were the last man on earth. She wouldn't give a damn about him if she were the only woman and he were. . .

'The door won't open,' she said.

'What?'

'The door is stuck,' she said, rattling the knob in frustration.

His voice was lazy. 'Have you unhooked the chain latch?'

If she were a cat, she would have scratched out his eyes, but since she wasn't, Samantha had to fall back on sarcasm. 'No, I left the hook on. It's always easier to open doors with the hook on.'

'Try turning the bolt.'

Her voice raised a decibel. 'I *am* trying to turn it. It only goes half-way.'

'Don't get huffy,' he said blandly. 'Just give the door a good tug.'

She gave the door a good tug; in fact, she pulled with all her might, but it wouldn't budge. 'I told you,' she said, 'it's stuck.'

Josh gave a theatrical groan as he stood up. 'Why is it,' he asked, 'that women suffer from the delusion that they're equal to men?'

'Not equal,' she said coldly as he came up beside her. 'Superior.'

'Oh?' he said, raising an eyebrow.

'We may not be stronger, but we're smarter.'

Josh gave the door a tug. 'That's questionable.'

Samantha noted with satisfaction that the door didn't budge at all. 'We're more intuitive, more understanding about people, more sensitive.'

He pulled again. 'You think men are insensitive?'

The door remained shut. 'Yes.'

Another pull, harder this time, making the muscles in his forearms bulge. 'Is this based on personal experience or just an outside judgment?'

She was beginning to love that door. 'Both,' she said smugly.

'Well,' said Josh, standing back from the door and eyeing it from top to bottom, 'I think we're locked in.'

Samantha's smugness evaporated. She didn't want to be locked into a stateroom with Joshua Sinclair. She wanted out. 'What do you mean—locked in?'

'There's something wrong with the bolt, I suspect. We'll have to wait for the purser to let us out.'

She was starting to feel frantic. 'Can't we call him?'

'Sure,' he gestured towards the phone, 'if you can reach him.'

By the time he was back at the couch, Samantha had already discovered that the purser's line was busy. By the time Josh had plumped up the cushion and discarded his shirt altogether, she'd figured out that there was little chance that the line would *not* be busy. And, by the time he had settled himself into a position of comfort with his ankles crossed and his eyes closed, Samantha had realised that there wasn't a chance in hell that she was going to get through to the purser for a good long time.

For a brief second, she considered the possibility of standing at the door and banging on it with her fists and screaming at the top of her lungs, but that did seem a bit excessive when you considered the fact that she was locked into a luxurious stateroom with a bed, a bathroom, a fully equipped drinks cabinet and a generously packed fruit basket. On the other hand, she was enclosed in a small space, against her will, with a strange man whose sexual inclinations just might be dangerous. Who knew what he was capable of? Samantha leaned her head against the traitorous door and let her imagination run riot. She had an instant and vivid vision of Josh forcefully taking her in his arms, locking her against that broad bare chest, his dark head bending as his mouth descended to take hers. She imagined his hand, the one that had brushed so lightly against her breasts, unzipping the long zipper that ran down the back of her dress, his warm fingers running down the length of her sensitive spine. She imagined. . .

Good God, what was she doing! Samantha straightened up, blinked and wondered what was the matter with her. Was she going out of her mind? Was she losing her grasp of reality? It was too ridiculous. She disliked Josh intensely, didn't she? And she wasn't some adolescent girl who spent her time indulging in silly fantasies. She was a woman of thirty, an accredited lawyer, a sensible and logical person who didn't let her imagination run away from her.

'Well,' she said, taking a deep breath and turning around, 'so here we are.'

But there was no answer from the body lying prone on the couch, merely a breathing so calm and so deep that Samantha realised her would-be rapist was sound asleep, completely and maddeningly indifferent to her presence.

CHAPTER THREE

TWENTY minutes later, Samantha and Josh were in the act of being freed by an apologetic steward. It was a long and infuriating twenty minutes from Samantha's point of view—since she had nothing to do but read, wander between the sitting room and the bedroom, stare out of the porthole or gaze at a sleeping Josh. But, no matter what she did, she found she was drawn to the sitting room. By the time she did get through to the purser's office she had quite memorised the bone and musculature of Josh's torso. She knew how the skin curved over the bulge of his shoulder muscles, how it indented to a pulsing hollow in his throat, how it stretched across the width of his chest, its colour bronzed and smooth beneath the mat of curly dark hair.

Finally, in sheer desperation, she shut herself away in the bedroom. Not that that did much good, since every few minutes she'd have to go into the sitting room and try to call the purser, at which point she would find, once again, that she was staring at Josh.

So it was with great relief that she finally did get through to the purser's office and, while she didn't actually reach the purser, she did catch one steward who was quite horrified to hear that not only was she locked into her stateroom, but that she was also sharing it with a stranger. Josh awoke during this conversation, looking as fresh as a daisy, stretched luxuriously and announced that he was going to take a shower. So he wasn't around for the anxious minutes while the steward discovered that he couldn't open the door either and rushed off to find the crew's handyman. He only showed up later when the door was being removed from its hinges, arriving in the sitting room wearing only a brief white towel wrapped around his hips, his hair damp and curling on his forehead.

'Just in time for dinner,' he said.

Samantha glanced at him and then quickly looked away. She refused, absolutely refused, to contemplate the long, lean and muscular legs of a man who obviously kept himself extremely fit.

'I guess so,' she said glumly.

'Are you in the first seating for dinner, too?'

She picked up her room assignment from the table and glanced at it. 'Yes,' she said. 'Six o'clock to seven—table four.'

Josh gave her a sarcastic grin. 'Too bad—I'm at table six.'

'Hmm,' she said, her eyes on the door, watching as it shook slightly on its hinges.

'Why, Miss Lorimer,' he said idly, walking over and making himself comfortable on the couch, 'I do believe our enforced intimacy is getting to you.'

He was far too close to her for comfort, although there was nowhere Samantha could go in that small room to get away from him. He was so close that she could smell the pleasing scent of his cologne, and if she turned around, those legs would practically be touching her own. The thought of it not only made her head swim slightly, but it also made her angry. She despised her own weakness and was furious with Josh for making her feel that way.

'Look,' she said, turning to face him, 'let's get this straight, all right? I came on this vacation to get away from problems and stress and aggravation. And I like my privacy. My idea of a holiday does not include being shut in with a stranger that I don't know and the little that I do know I don't . . .' She paused, stopping the rush of angry words, not wanting to say the words hovering at the tip of her tongue.

'Don't like?' Josh asked casually, and it was obvious that he really didn't care what Samantha thought of him.

'Yes,' she said, lifting her chin. 'So they can't get me out of here fast enough.'

'You know, Miss . . . you don't mind if I call you Samantha, do you? . . . You know, Samantha, you've really got to learn to relax and roll with the punches. You're too uptight.'

Great—now they were going to make value judgments on her personality. 'I am,' she said, making a valiant effort to match her mood to her words, 'even and calm-tempered.'

He laughed; one could even say that he roared with laughter, throwing his head back and letting the sounds rise to the ceiling. Samantha glared at him and then turned haughtily away. She hated him; the word 'dislike' didn't begin to describe how she felt about him. In fact, she had never quite felt about anyone the way she now felt about Joshua Sinclair. Certainly no one had ever inspired a feeling so deep and so passionate that she was actually trembling inside with fury and rage.

She was never quite sure what would have happened then—she did want to commit murder—if the door hadn't finally broken off its hinges. There was a loud, cracking sound, then the door opened from the wrong side and the anxious face of the steward appeared. Profuse apologies were the order of day, with the steward wringing his hands in distress and Samantha assuring him that she was fine and Josh ignoring it all and leaving to get dressed. What finally emerged was that the door would be fixed immediately and that the purser would like to see Josh and Samantha in his office after dinner—at which point, the steward assured her, they would have managed to straighten out this unfortunate mess, that in all the history of the Vulcan Cruise Line there had never been such a slip-up, that he couldn't imagine what had gone wrong, it must be that new computer system, but he could assure her, and he'd stake his professional reputation on it, that it would never happen again and. . .

'As long as I have my own room by tonight,' Samantha said soothingly, 'I'll be fine.'

'Oh, madam, without a doubt. Please don't worry about it. And Mr Sinclair, we'll have him fixed up as well. Please tell him not to be concerned.'

Samantha turned to the closed bedroom door and waved a hand towards it. From behind it was the sound of cheerful whistling. 'I doubt,' she said with a touch of irony, 'if Mr Sinclair even gives a damn.'

The dining room of the *Princess Marguerita* was large and pleasantly appointed. The tables were all set with crisp white linen and cut-glass vases holding red carnations. One wall held a wide window that overlooked one of the ship's pleasure decks and, beyond that, the turquiose waters of the Mediterranean. The other walls were decorated with colourful posters of Greek cities and ports. The waiters and waitresses were efficient, the menu choices were varied and the diners appeared to be having a terrific time. At Samantha's table were two married couples who had immediately got into a conversation about the children they'd left back home, and a woman in her late twenties, who hailed from a small town in South Carolina.

'. . . Mariposa, South Carolina, to be precise,' she said. Her name was Marybeth McMullen, she had a soft Southern accent and one of those engaging faces that you can't help liking on sight. It was round with a slightly pointed chin and framed in short, blonde curls. She had a sprinkling of freckles along a narrow, diminutive nose and big blue eyes that reflected every emotion that she was feeling. Right now that emotion was eager curiosity. 'How about you?'

'New York City,' said Samantha.

'I would give my right arm to live in New York City,' Marybeth said with a sigh. '*Anything* would be better than Mariposa. It has a population of five thousand and most of that's my family. That's why I came on this cruise. I just had to get away and meet some new people or I thought I'd go absolutely batty.' She gave a little laugh. 'Heavens, but I'm running on! What do you do, Samantha?'

'I'm a lawyer and work for a firm doing mostly real estate law.'

'A *lawyer*,' said Marybeth with awe. 'Why, I bet you just whizzed through school. I wish I could have been the intellectual type, but I was just plain hopeless!'

Samantha smiled. 'Being intellectual isn't everything.'

'Any boyfriends?'

'Not right now.'

'Why, I'd think you'd meet *piles* of exciting men in a lawyer's office.'

'Attached, married or senile,' Samantha said drily, thinking of the partners in her firm.

Marybeth laughed. 'And before?'

Samantha shrugged. 'Someone from law school—but it didn't last.'

Marybeth might have loved gossip and secrets and the stories of past intimacies, but she apparently knew better than to press Samantha any further. She just sighed in commiseration as if she too knew all about the agonies and traumas of broken affairs and said gloomily, 'Well, I can tell you all about my love life in two seconds—there's so little of it and I'm so pure, the deacons of our church are thinking of immortalising me in stained glass. Why, I could tell you stories about dull dates and boring men until the cows fly home. That's why I saved my pennies so I could take this cruise.'

'You think you're going to meet someone on this cruise?'

Marybeth's blue eyes were dreamy. 'I sure hope so—isn't that why singles go on cruises anyway? I'd just like to have a wild, romantic fling with no holds barred. You know the kind I mean?'

Samantha didn't know, not really. Her relationships with men had always been very careful, very logical, very organised. And as for her first and last lover—well, what could you expect when two neophyte lawyers decide to have an affair? Their passion had been muted; their caution had been great. On the other hand, she wasn't any different from any other woman who had been brought up on a steady diet of television, movies and novels. In an abstract way, she knew exactly what Marybeth was talking about.

'Uh-uh,' she said.

But Marybeth was no longer listening. '... and dance under the stars and take walks under the moonlight and have sexy sweet nothings whispered in my ear. Of course, he'll have to be tall and handsome and sophisticated.' She laughed and came down to earth. 'I don't want too much, do I? Do you know any men like that?'

'Nope,' Samantha said.

Marybeth heaved a dramatic sigh. 'Me neither.'

'Maybe they don't exist.'

'Gosh, Samantha, you gotta keep on dreaming. If you didn't have your dreams, what would you have?'

Their dessert arrived at that moment, a concoction whipped up of strawberries and cake and whipped cream. Samantha stared down at it instead of answering Marybeth's question. Once she had dreamed romantic fantasies just like the one Marybeth proposed, but as the years went by, she'd given up on it. She no longer really believed that such dreams could be true; they belonged to the realm of girlish nonsense, to wishful thinking, to an imagination that hadn't yet been stifled by reality. *If you didn't have your dreams, what would you have*? Nothing, she wanted to say, nothing but work and a certain cynicism that extinguished every little flicker of hope and crushed dreams before they ever had a chance to get started.

'Well,' said Marybeth gaily, taking a final lick of her whipped cream, 'We can start tonight.'

'Doing what?'

'Fulfilling our dreams.'

Samantha wished she had just the tiniest bit of Marybeth's unquenchable optimism, but it wasn't in her nature to believe that one could fulfil one's dreams on demand. 'And how,' she asked wryly, 'are we going to do that?'

Marybeth gave her a disbelieving look. 'At the dance, of course.'

'What dance?'

'Didn't you read the schedule?'

'I never saw a schedule. I was locked into my room.'

'Locked into your room?!'

'The door wouldn't work.'

'Good grief, Samantha, that would only be worthwhile if you were stuck in there with a tall, dark and handsome stranger.'

Samantha took a sip of her coffee. 'I was.'

Marybeth had been about to drink her own coffee, but now she put the cup down with a clatter. 'You what?' she demanded.

'I was stuck in the room with a tall, dark and handsome stranger.'

'Heavens,' said Marybeth admiringly, 'you are a fast worker.'

Samantha could see that she was going to have to nip Marybeth's over-active imagination in the bud. 'We were put together by mistake. Besides, I didn't like him,' she said. 'And he didn't like me.'

'That's too bad.' Marybeth looked around the room. 'Is he here?'

He was, and Samantha knew exactly where. 'Behind me, two tables down, facing us.'

Marybeth craned her neck and glimpsed down the aisle with a blatant curiosity. 'Does he have dark brown hair?'

'Yes.'

'And dark eyes?'

'Yes.'

Marybeth straightened up. 'Why, Samantha, he's gorgeous!'

'Yes,' Samantha said reluctantly.

'Are you absolutely sure, I mean completely convinced that you don't like him?'

'Absolutely.'

'Hmm,' said Marybeth, giving Josh another glance with the appraising eye of a woman who is looking over a potential acquisition. 'Is he hooked up with a redhead?'

'Redhead?'

'Strawberry blonde, elegant, manicured nails, about thirty-five.'

Samantha couldn't bear it any longer. She turned around to follow Marybeth's glance—and then was sorry she'd done so. There was Josh all right, looking extremely handsome in a blue velour pullover and an open-necked white shirt. Beside him was a woman who was just as Marybeth described her. She had a model's slim elegance, reddish-gold hair that was coiled on her head, and the sort of high-cheekboned face that would launch a thousand ships. And she was obviously fascinated by Josh's conversation. On top of that, she had the rapacious look of a woman who has a good-looking man within her grasp and fully intends to keep him there. Samantha turned back and concentrated with great intensity on her dessert.

'Well,' said Marybeth, 'I'm not the only one who's out for a shipboard romance, that's for sure.' She glanced once more towards Josh and his dinner companion and then heaved her largest sigh of the evening. 'And the competition's going to be fierce—very, very fierce!'

Samantha left the dining room soon after that, said goodbye to Marybeth, who planned on taking a long time to put her warpaint on for the dance that night, and took a slow leisurely walk towards the purser's office. It wasn't seven o'clock yet, so she couldn't be sure that the purser would be ready to see her. Besides, he would probably want to talk to Josh as well, and since Josh was busily occupied in the dining room, Samantha figured she had about a half an hour of free time to kill.

So she wandered around the upper decks of the ship, thinking about shipboard romances and wondering if she really wanted one. Part of her yearned for romance, for love, for all the clichés that movies and novels are made of. Margaret had thought she was too stuffy to accept the gift of the purchased fantasy, but the truth was that, underneath, Samantha was far too romantic. She didn't want a man who'd been paid to court her, nor did she want a man who would woo her, knowing that they'd be parting in two weeks' time. No, Samantha thought, she wasn't like Marybeth who had saved her pennies in the hopes of finding an exotic, short-lived thrill.

She was so engrossed in this analysis that she walked headlong into a slim and wiry man who was turning the corner at precisely the same moment that she was.

'Excuse me,' she said breathlessly.

He smiled at her, and the smile turned a rather plain face into a charming one, crinkling up the corners of the blue eyes and revealing a strong set of white teeth.

'Excuse *me*,' he said. 'I wasn't watching where I was going.'

'That's gallant of you to take the blame,' Samantha smiled, 'but it was really my fault.'

He smiled again.

'I'm David Burroughs, by the way. And just to make the introductions less tedious—I live in Washington, work for a Senator, have never been married and like swimming, squash, white water rafting, good cooking and a hefty biography. Now it's your turn.'

Samantha couldn't help laughing. 'Well,' she told him, 'my name is Samantha Lorimer and I live in New York where I practise law and take care of two cats. I've never been married either.'

'Whew! That solves that,' said David, mopping his forehead in mock-relief. 'Now we can get on to other, more important issues.'

'Like what?'

'Political inclinations, sociological aspirations, metaphysical opinions and whether you're going to the dance or not tonight.'

Samantha had decided that she liked David Burroughs. She liked his smiling blue eyes, his sense of humour, and the way his brown hair fell forward on his forehead. 'The dance, yes,' she said. 'I'm afraid you'll have to repeat the rest. I forgot it.'

He grinned at her. 'That makes two of us!'

From there, the conversation was easy and light and pleasant. As they ambled down the ship's corridors, Samantha learned that David had been a political science major in college who was now part of the vast Federal Government, working as an analyst in the Department of Health and Wealfare, monitoring medical regulations. This particular holiday was the first time he'd tried a cruise, but work had been so hectic that he'd decided that it would be better to relax than try to hike up another mountain in Nepal or ski down the Swiss Alps.

'And what about you?' he asked. 'What got you on to the *Princess Marguerita*?'

Samantha was about to explain when a deep voice interrupted her. 'So there you are!'

She whirled around to find Josh approaching her. 'I was. . .' she began.

'Darling,' he said, smiling down at her and taking her arm, 'I've been looking for you.'

Samantha's mouth dropped open in shock. 'Dar. . .?'

'Sweetheart,' he purred, 'we have an appointment. Did you forget?'

Sweetheart? Since when was she his sweetheart? And there was David, looking confused, and she couldn't blame him. After all, he had thought she was a single, unattached woman, and along came a stranger and acted as if the two of them were a well-established couple. What was Josh up to anyway?

Samantha tried to disengage her arm from his grasp. 'If you don't mind!' she protested.

But he was ignoring her and offering his other hand to David. 'Josh Sinclair,' he said pleasantly.

David shook hands with him. 'David Burroughs.'

'Thanks for keeping Samantha occupied,' Josh said, 'but we have an appointment with the purser.'

'That's okay,' David said, but he was frowning and he kept looking from Samantha to Josh and then back again in total bewilderment.

'So, if you'll excuse us. . .'

David's frown deepened, but he was too much the gentleman to do anything but acquiesce. 'Sure,' he said.

'Now, just a minute!' Samantha began hotly, but it was too late. Josh had manoeuvred her away from David and was now propelling her rapidly down the corridor. 'Cut it out!'

'But, darling, we have an appointment.'

She struggled to free herself from Josh's grasp, but he was holding on to her with a firm grip. 'Don't darling me,' she retorted. 'And let go!'

'Samantha, you're letting yourself get hot under the collar again.'

Was he crazy? Or course she was getting hot under the collar. Who wouldn't be in her position? He'd kidnapped her—that's what he'd done, virtually kidnapped her in broad daylight. Well, amend that—under the fluorescent lamps in the corridor. But still, he'd interrupted her while she was having a very nice discussion with a very nice and perfectly eligible man, talked to her as if they were. . . well, lovers, for heaven's sake, and then forcibly abducted her.

'I'd like to know what you're up to,' she said through clenched teeth.

'Up to?' he asked innocently.

'All those darlings and sweethearts. You know what that sounded like?'

'What?'

'Like we were in the midst of an. . . affair!'

Josh slowed down a bit and looked down at her. 'Us? You and me?' He threw his head back and laughed. 'Samantha, you're letting your imagination run away with you.'

'I am not!'

'Who would imagine us having an affair? We're totally incompatible.'

'David doesn't know that.'

He gave her a quick glance. 'You're interested in David?'

'I. . . it's none of your business!' How had Josh managed to manoeuvre her into a discussion of her feelings about David? Samantha's eyes narrowed and she gave one strong final yank of her arm, almost falling over when he let it go.

'Are you all right?' he asked in what she considered overly solicitous tones.

'Of course I'm all right,' she said tartly, brushing her bare arm and looking to see if he'd given her bruises. Much to Samantha's annoyance, there wasn't a mark on her which could be used as evidence of Josh's brutality. 'And I would prefer it if you didn't ever treat me that way again.'

'Treat you how?'

'As if. . .' But what could she say? Samantha thought in angry frustration, letting her words die away. From his expression of polite bewilderment, you would have thought that Josh hadn't deviated one single inch from normal correct behaviour.

'Here we are,' he said, ushering her through an open door. 'The purser's office.'

The purser, a tall balding man with wire-rimmed spectacles, was even more apologetic than the steward had been. As he had them sit down beside his desk, he said how sorry he'd been for the mix-up, the inconvenience, the upset they must have suffered. He and the captain and the management of Vulcan Cruises begged them to please understand that this was the first time anything so bizarre had ever occurred, and that they would do everything in their power to ensure that both Miss Lorimer and Mr Sinclair were made comfortable and happy.

Samantha was attempting to soothe her ruffled feathers while this barrage of words poured over her. She was still fuming inside over Josh's high-handed actions, and every once in a while she'd throw him a furious glance. Not that her angry looks made much of an impression on him. He was leaning back in his chair with his arms crossed over his chest, nodding slightly and looking for all the world as if he had nothing more important on his mind than the purser's apologies.

'Now, of course,' he was saying, 'this accident occurred because of an over-booking error. For some reason our computer accepted one more reservation than was available, and one of the secretaries compounded the error by putting the two of you together in a room. The problem is,' he coughed a bit and cleared his throat, 'that the over-booking still exists, however, and at this very moment. . .'

By now, Samantha had focused on the purser. 'Are you saying,' she said, leaning forward, 'that we're still going to have to share a stateroom?'

The purser looked distinctly uncomfortable. 'Miss Lorimer, I'm sure you'll understand our problem. Every available space on board is taken and. . .'

'For the *entire* trip?'

The purser was a hand-wringer, too. 'Of course, we'll reimburse you for the difference between a single accommodation and a double and throw in something extra for the inconvenience.'

'But there's only one bed!'

'No, no, the couch turns into a bed, Miss Lorimer. Heavens, we wouldn't expect. . .' the purser gave a small, embarrassed laugh, 'that you would. . . er. . . sleep together.'

Samantha slumped in her chair. 'I don't believe this,' she said heavily.

'Of course, if someone gets ill and leaves the cruise, we'll move you right away. The same if anyone decides to leave the cruise at one of the ports. It's also possible that you could share a room with another woman, but I'm afraid we won't know that for a while. We'll have to keep our ears to the ground to see if there's someone who would like a room-mate to keep down expenses. Of course, if you make friends with. . .'

But Samantha wasn't stupid; she could see the writing on the wall. 'I can't believe this is happening to me!' she gasped.

At which point Josh grinned, uncurled himself from the chair where he'd been relaxing, leaned over and gave her a soothing pat on the arm. 'That's all right, darling. You'll see—it'll be like a dream come true.'

CHAPTER FOUR

SAMANTHA did manage to get out of the purser's office without throwing a temper tantrum, but it wasn't easy. She marched down to her stateroom, slammed the newly installed door and threw herself down on to the couch in a state of fury and frustration. Dream come true, indeed—he had a hell of a nerve! As if there was any chance that she'd happily reconcile herself to living with him, much less consider herself lucky to be with a man who obviously thought himself God's gift to womankind. Samantha couldn't imagine any way that she could find contentment in being near a man so odious and loathsome. And he hadn't cared! That was the part that really killed her. Josh really hadn't cared whether he shared a room with her or not. She was the one who was flouncing around, making angry statements and working herself into a frenzy.

Was she being unreasonable? Samantha awkwardly swallowed that thought as if she had eaten something unsavoury and lumpy. Well, she didn't much like to admit it, but she reluctantly conceded that she'd not had a relaxed, roll-with-the-punches attitude. She'd ranted and raved, she'd fumed and stewed, and what good had it done? Nothing she had said would alter the situation, no matter how unpalatable it was. She really had no choice, she saw, except to yield graciously and, as the saying went, put the best face on a bad situation. Besides, she might never again have the opportunity to cruise through the Greek Islands, and she really didn't want to ruin her trip by being sulky and down-in-the-mouth.

So she stood up, shook herself slightly and decided to dress for the dance. She had so many new clothes, she wasn't sure what to choose first. The styles ranged from sweet and demure to sexy and vampy. There was a strapless red dress with a flared skirt, a pale yellow with a prim neckline and a plunging back and, most glamorous of all, one with a gold-sequined top and a slim black skirt that had a kick pleat on the side that went up the length of her leg. Margaret had chosen that one.

There was a knock on the door at that moment, and she opened it to find Marybeth standing there in all her evening finery.

'You look wonderful,' Samantha said, letting her in. 'What a lovely dress!'

'Thank you, honeybunch,' smiled Marybeth, swirling around so that Samantha could get a full view of a frothy aquamarine confection that dipped low in front, swooped to the waist at the back and showed Marybeth's petite but full figure off to its best advantage. 'And how come you're not dressed yet? The dance starts in fifteen minutes.'

Samantha glanced at her watch and groaned. 'I just came from a visit to the purser. It seems he can't change my room.

Marybeth made herself at home on a chair, crossing her silk-sheathed legs and letting her foot swing in its high-heeled white sandal. 'You mean you're stuck in this room with that gorgeous man?'

Samantha had a brainstorm. 'Marybeth, I know this is an awful thing to ask, but is there any chance I could move in with you?'

'Why, Samantha, I'd love it, but I have a single room in the bilge. There's hardly enough room there to swing a cat.'

'Oh,' Samantha said with a sigh, then made one last effort. 'I don't suppose you'd like to change places.'

Marybeth blinked her big blue eyes. 'You mean— move in here?'

Samantha warmed to it. 'Why not? You wanted a shipboard romance and this would be a ready-made setting. Besides, you did think Josh was awfully good-looking and. . .'

Marybeth was shaking her head. 'I'm not very neat,' she said.

Samantha waved that aside. 'Josh wouldn't mind.'

'And he already has the redhead hot on his trail. Samantha honey, I wish I could help you, I really do, but I think I'd rather stay where I am.'

Samantha couldn't blame her. What woman in her right mind would give up her privacy to room with a stranger—and a male one at that? 'That's okay. It was a stupid idea anyway.'

'Besides, maybe you'll find you do like him after all.'

Samantha sighed. 'There's not much chance of that. When I'm with him, it's like trying to mix oil and water.'

'Well,' said Marybeth, her natural optimism returning, 'the best thing to do is get yourself dolled up for the dance and have a wonderful time.'

'Right,' said Samantha, standing up, 'that's just what I plan to do.'

But her plans were thwarted when the door opened then and Josh walked in. He didn't look the least put out to find Marybeth there. In fact, if anything, he seemed quite entranced by Marybeth's blonde prettiness, the deep V of her décolletage and her pleasing Southern voice. Actually, it might have been Samantha's imagination, but from the moment of Josh's entrance, Marybeth's accent had deepened to the point that one could almost smell the wafting scent of magnolias in the room, and it occurred to her that Marybeth's arrival in her room had a deeper motive than mere female friendship.

'... and where's home, Mr Sinclair?' asked Marybeth, after the introductions had been made.

'New York City.'

'Why, isn't that amazing! That's Samantha's home town, too.'

'Is it?' Josh asked and glanced at Samantha.

'It is, isn't it, Samantha?'

'Yes,' Samantha said coolly, not particularly relishing the idea that she and Josh had anything in common. '93rd Street, actually.'

Josh had leaned back on the sofa, put an ankle over one knee and his arm nonchalantly along the back of the couch. '93rd and what?'

'Riverside Drive.'

'Interesting,' he said. 'I'm at 99th and Riverside.'

Marybeth clapped her hands. 'Imagine—you two are neighbours!'

'Not exactly,' Samantha said quickly.

'But only six blocks apart,' Marybeth said. 'And to think that you had to meet in Greece! Now that's really ironic, isn't it?'

'Very,' Josh agreed drily, and Samantha gave him a quick sideways glance. But his face had no other expression on it than a pleasant good humour.

'Samantha did tell me all about this mix-up with your room.' Marybeth went on. 'And it sounds just horrendous. I mean, imagine coming on a cruise and expecting to have your privacy and finding out that you have to sleep with a stranger.' Her eyes widened, and she put her small hand in front of her mouth. 'Oops—now, why on earth did I put it that way?'

'I don't know, Marybeth,' he said teasingly, 'why on earth did you?'

It was clear to Samantha that Marybeth couldn't resist a flirtation. 'Why, Mr Sinclair. . .' the other woman began, her eyelashes fluttering.

'Josh.'

'Why, Josh, it must have been your presence that threw my mind into such disarray.'

It was more than Samantha could take. Not that she had any reason to resent Marybeth's blatant flirting with Josh, she told herself. After all, she'd certainly let the other woman know just how much she disliked him, and that left the field wide open for anyone, Marybeth included, to step right in and see how far she could go. Still, it was ovious that her nerves were still raw from the rest of the day's happenings, and Marybeth, Southern belle extraordinaire, combined with an affable and flirtatious Josh, was just a little more than her fragile temperament could handle right at the moment.

So she stood up again with determinationand said, 'If you two don't mind, I'd like to get dressed for the dance.'

Josh merely grinned at her, stood up and offered Marybeth his arm. 'Why don't I take you for a drink and let Samantha have the room to herself? I can get dressed when she's done.'

Marybeth looked tiny and feminine when she stood beside Josh's tall, lean figure. She had to tilt her head way back to look up at him. 'I'd love a drink,' she said, and tucked her small, plump hand in his arm.

They were laughing gaily as they left the state-room, and Samantha looked at the closed door with a sour look. Then she shook herself hard and, walking into the bedroom, threw open the door to the closet. She ran her hand over the sleeve of the pale yellow dress, fingered the organdie of the red and then pushed them both aside. With narrowed eyes, she contemplated the gold and black dress, imagining herself in it, remembering the way it had looked on her in the department store. Sexy and vampy, that was how she'd looked. Like a siren looking for seduction. Like a woman out on the make.

Not that she was, of course. Samantha had never been out on the make in her life and didn't have the audacity to think that she'd carry it off any better at the ripe old age of thirty than she had at sixteen when she'd gone to her first high school dance in a tight red dress that her mother had thought hideous, her nails lacquered a regrettable shade of purple, and her face plastered with make-up borrowed from a friend. Despite all her efforts, however, her appearance had not brought the boys running: it had only served to make her the most colourful wallflower in that hot and humid school gymnasium.

Samantha had learned her lesson from that experience: it had haunted her for years and had kept her in a wardrobe that was marked by pragmatism, efficiency and sensible colours. She'd actually been shocked when Margaret had pulled the gold and black dress off the rack and flourished it in the air like a matador's cape. Samantha had immediately protested: it wasn't her, it was cut too low in the front, it was cut too high on the leg. Margaret had, in her usual manner, ignored everything Samantha had said and insisted that she try it on. The effect had been quite mesmerising. Samantha hadn't known that she possessed such curves.

Perhaps, she thought as she ran her fingers over the sparkling edges of the gold sequins, perhaps the moment had come to close the door on the past and admit that she was no longer sixteen-year-old, awkward and gawky Samantha Lorimer. It was really quite possible, given Margaret's taste and some courage on her part, that she might actually turn out to be someone quite different. Who exactly? Well, not her lawyerlike self, that person she'd known for years, but another kind of a woman, the sort who attracted the curious, interested looks of men, whose mouth invited kisses under the moonlight, whose. . .

Get a hold of yourself! There was no point in wishing for the moon, Samantha thought wryly. Let's not forget the facts. Even the most fabulous dress in the world wasn't going to change her, miraculously, into a movie star or world-famous model. She would still be Samantha Lorimer, the kind of ordinary woman that men liked as a friend, an acquaintance, a business partner. So there was no point in getting stars in her eyes and deluding herself with sentimental, romantic dreams. On the other hand, for some reason, the opening dance of the cruise had taken on a special significance for her, she couldn't say just what exactly, but it seemed exceedingly important that she enter that ballroom, dressed to kill. *And just who is the intended victim?* a small voice inside her asked. She stared at the dress and wondered. It certainly wasn't David who, nice though he was, didn't even start her pulses fluttering. And it certainly wasn't Josh. She couldn't stand him, for heaven's sake, and she couldn't have cared less about what he thought or did. So who did that leave?

Who precisely did that leave?

Josh was instantly aware that he wasn't the only man in the bar to notice the woman who had walked in. There was a swivelling of heads, a dip in the general noise level and, if you listened closely, a slight intake of about twenty breaths in unison. The object of this second of concerted appreciation appeared to be totally ignorant of the impression that she was making. Josh sat at an angle to the door and therefore had not seen her face, but her walk alone would have caught his attention. It was a straight-shouldered, swaying-hipped, head-up walk, the kind that is made particularly attractive when its owner is wearing black high heels that emphasise slender, shapely calves, a black skirt with a slit up the side that reveals tantalisingly brief glimpses of thigh, and a glittering gold bodice whose strapless back dipped low enough to expose a delicate spine, curved white shoulders and a deliciously soft nape.

He gave the back of this woman so much of his concentration that he was oblivious to Marybeth beside him who was chattering on about her vacation last year, '. . . the same cottage on the same lake—why, I tell you, a person can only take so much. . .' For a moment, Josh had actually thought that the woman was Nadja: she had the same autocratic angle of head, the same sexy walk, the same proud angle of shoulder, but then he realised his mistake. Nadja had long, dark hair that she wore in a coil on her head: this woman had short, dark curls, she was not as tall, she wasn't quite as thin. He shook his head in irritation. *Forget her.* He'd told himself

that a million times since the break-up. A million
times.

He hadn't even loved Nadja, he'd realised that
later, but he couldn't help the bitter residue of the
affair. Bud had been right about her, she'd been
amusing herself with a working man, jetting in from
Paris to be with him at weekends, going with him to
restaurants that he could afford, declaring that she
loved walks in cold and snowy Central Park when
she'd just come off the ski slopes of St Moritz. Of
course, it hadn't lasted. The fact was, Josh hadn't
even been surprised when it was over.

'. . . and I said to myself, Marybeth honey, it's
time to treat yourself. It's time to stop sacrificing
yourself for the common family good. Now, I knew
that was selfish, but I simply couldn't *bear* the idea
of spending another two weeks with my brother and
sister-in-law. Not that I don't love them. I do,
but. . .'

The woman had walked the length of the bar to
the entrance of the ballroom and then turned, as if
she were undecided about entering. She was just as
tempting, Josh noticed, from the front as from
behind. She had smooth, curved hips beneath the
black satin, firm high breasts that did justice to the
revealing neckline, a slender, delicate face beneath
gleaming dark curls and. . .

Good God, but it was Samantha!

'Josh honey, are you listening to me?'

'What?—yes, of course I am.'

Samantha changed her mind again, turned back
to the entrance of the ballroom and walked in.

The voice was very Southern. 'I could have sworn
you were *miles* away.'

Josh looked at Marybeth's eager face with its big
blue eyes and pouting mouth. 'No, I wasn't,' he said

gently. 'I was right here in the room with you.'

Actually, Samantha's nerve had just about abandoned her. Perhaps it was the hurtful memory of that high school gymnasium with its paper flower decorations and her own unfulfilled adolescent fantasies. Or perhaps it was simply the cold and sobering realisation that she was, without escort, about to walk into a party where she knew no one and might not even like the company, a situation that would make even the most confident of adults feel the slightest bit shaky. Whatever it was, her normal poise practically deserted her, and rather than enter the ballroom through its main entrance, she had ducked into the darkened atmosphere of the bar and walked quickly through it without noticing who was there.

For a brief second, panic overcame every emotion, and Samantha turned to head back to the safe and quite haven of her stateroom. Then, just as quickly as it had overtaken her, the panic subsided and her usual composure returned. What precisely was she afraid of? she asked herself with disgust. Being a wallflower again? Well, suppose she was. Just suppose it happened to her again. Would it make any difference in her life?

With that thought, she turned back, walked determinedly into the ballroom and headed towards one of the bars, even though she'd never been much of a drinker. She joined a line-up at the bar and turned to watch the band, relaxing a bit and liking their sound, feeling the beat of the music echoing in her own pulse.

'Well, we meet again,' a male voice said in cool tones.

Samantha turned to find David standing behind

her. He was wearing a white dinner jacket and blue slacks and, although the colours suited him, she was struck once again by how plain he looked when he wasn't smiling. And of course, she knew precisely why he wasn't smiling. She knew what lay behind his watchful, cautious glance and his less-than-enthusiastic welcome.

'David,' she said brightly, 'how are you?'

But he didn't respond to her smile. 'Fine,' he said flatly, his eyes looking behind her and then to her side. 'What happened to your friend?'

'He's not a friend.'

'No, I guessed that.'

'No, you have it all wrong,' she said with a little laugh to show him that she hadn't taken any offence at his innuendo. 'Josh is someone I'm sharing a stateroom with—by *mistake*,' she hastened to add.

The line moved forward. 'Mistake?'

'It sounds ridiculous. I know, but we were put into the same stateroom through a computer error, and we're stuck there for the moment. I never knew Josh before. We were complete strangers.'

'Really?' His smile was disbelieving, and Samantha remembered all those 'darlings' and 'sweethearts' that Josh had spread so liberally around during that ill-fated meeting.

'Really,' she said, and laid her hand on David's sleeve jacket as if by her touch she could convince him. 'I know the way he sounded, but it was a joke. He's a . . .' she sought for the right words and came up with, ' . . . a practical joker.'

Perhaps it was her hand lying lightly on his arm or her earnest face that got through to him, but David visibly relaxed, a smile lighting up his blue eyes and making him seem boyish and almost handsome. 'Well, I was fooled all right,' he said slowly. 'I figured you two had come together.'

'Never!' Samantha said vehemently. 'I don't even like him.'

They had reached the bar by this time and gave their orders to the bartender for two gin and tonics. Then, when their drinks were made, they walked to David's table and joined a group of people who already knew one another from the dinner seating. Samantha was introduced to Reuben, a tall and dark electrical engineer from Iowa—'I'm divorced,' he said with a grin—Betty, a secretary from Florida who was pretty and plump—'Separated,' she announced—and Marvin, a balding insurance broker from Schenectady who said in a laconic voice, 'Never been hooked.'

They were all joking, of course, but Samantha could see that it was one of those singles' gatherings that she had always studiously avoided, where everyone feels it necessary to get their cards out on the table before they get down to serious socialising. It was precisely the sort of group that made Samantha very uncomfortable. She didn't like to talk to strangers about herself. She didn't like the way people looked at one another with curious, avid glances. And she absolutely hated that feeling she got from them that she was part of a large shopping bazaar where each member was both a purchaser and an item up for sale.

So she was thankful for David's company, even though his attitude towards her, now that he was assured that Josh didn't matter, was a bit more proprietorial of her than she liked. As the conversation around the table jumped from topic to topic, he began to lean closer and closer to her. He draped his arm over the back of her chair, and within minutes, his hand was resting on her bare shoulder.

She was seriously considering asking him to move it, when he asked her to dance.

'I'd love to,' she said with alacrity.

The small square in front of the band was now crowded with couples swaying to the music. Samantha let David pull her close to him so that their bodies met, shoulder to shoulder, thigh to thigh. It was silly, she supposed, that she should feel more comfortable dancing intimately with him than when she was sitting next to him and his hand had lain on her shoulder. But then dancing, no matter how close, was conventional, accepted, casual, while that hand lying on her skin had been an uncomfortable statement about possession and ownership.

A sudden jolt made her eyes fly open and she found herself looking into a pair of narrowed dark eyes.

Fortunately, David's head was turned, and the dance floor was so crowded that he didn't have the room to spin her round and find out who had bumped into them. So he was spared the sight of Samantha staring at Josh over his shoulder, and Josh staring at Samantha over the red-gold head of the woman in his arms. Samantha felt that unsmiling stare right down to her toes, and she shivered in the circle of David's arms.

David stopped humming along to the music. 'Cold?'

'No,' she said, thankful when he finally danced her into a corner where there was a slight break in the crowd. Josh disappeared from her view, and she closed her eyes once again, trying hard to erase the vision of him from her mind. He hated her, of that she was sure. That was what his look had said: that he didn't like her any more than she liked him. That he found her presence as repugnant as she found his. That he no more wanted to be her room-mate than she wanted to be his. He might have appeared to be affable and relaxed about her in front of the purser, but the truth had been laid bare in that silent look. She was an unpleasant irritation and damned annoyance, and her presence in his stateroom was going to ruin whatever plans he made. Samantha wasn't stupid; she knew very well that, if Josh had intentions of bedding the redhead in his arms, she was going to be in the way.

She discovered that she didn't like the idea of Josh sharing the stateroom with the willowy redhead. It made some part of her feel quite dreadful, angry and . . . and jealous. *Jealous*? That was ridiculous. She couldn't possibly be jealous, because she didn't give a damn who Josh spent his time with or who he slept with. He could bed down the whole ship for all she cared. So where did all that unexpected emotion come from? Samantha shifted uneasily in David's arms and then breathed a sigh of relief as the answer came to her. She wasn't jealous of Josh at all, she was merely being possessive about the stateroom. She didn't really want another woman spending time in what should have been her own private sanctuary. That explained the anger and that awful feeling in the pit of her stomach.

The evening grew more raucous as it went on. Marybeth joined the group, and they grew ever drunker and more flirtatious. Samantha tried hard to get into the partying mood, but the longer it went on, the less she found she could join in. So she watched, smiled occasionally, danced with David when he asked her, and flinched—whenever she caught sight of Josh glancing their way. He was still with the redhead, she noticed, and they'd grown quite cosy. It was really quite nauseating the way that woman liked to encircle her arms around Josh's neck when they were dancing.

Finally, when she could take it no longer, Samantha rose and said she was tired and had to go to bed. There was a chorus of 'no' and 'please stay' and 'the best is yet to come', but she demurred and said she needed her beauty rest for tomorrow's stop at Mykonos. David insisted on walking her back to her stateroom and tucked his hand under her elbow as they wove their way through the tangle of revellers and tables. Samantha felt Josh's eyes following them, so she threw David a glittering smile and added an extra waggle to her hips. It was an adolescent thing to do, but she couldn't help herself and she'd already learned that, when it came to Josh, there seemed no point in fighting her overwhelming and often totally inexplicable impulses.

When she and David arrived at her stateroom door, she immediately realised that he wanted an invitation to go in with her, but she was quite firm about her intention of entering alone.

'Goodnight, David,' she said, opening the clasp of her bag and reaching for her key.

Fortunately, he was sensitive enough to not to push her. He merely gave a small, unconscious sigh and said, 'See you tomorrow at breakfast?'

'Fine,' she said, although her heart sank at the prospect of having to spend the whole of the next day with him. She didn't want to be paired off right away, and she was enough of a loner to look forward to sightseeing in Mykonos on her own.

'I had a great evening tonight.'

He was going to kiss her, she realised, and she gave him a wavering smile. 'I did, too.'

'We were good together.'

His mouth was drawing nearer. 'Yes, I guess we were.'

His head bent, and he began to draw her towards him. 'A little kiss to seal the evening?'

Samantha swallowed. 'Just a little one.'

He was smiling at her. 'And a promise of things to come.'

'I don't . . .' But it was too late, and he was kissing her, his lips quite firm against hers, his tongue licking at her lips. Samantha endured it as best she could, feeling immense relief when he lifted his head, let her go and said in a low voice laced with sexual innuendo, 'Goodnight, then.'

'Goodnight.'

And then he was gone, and Samantha sagged against the door to her stateroom as his figure disappeared around the corner of the corridor. What exactly had she got herself into? *A promise of things to come.* She had a sinking feeling that she knew exactly what sort of things David had in mind. And it was partly her fault, too. She'd been quite agreeable to spending the evening with him; she'd liked dancing with him and she'd liked talking to him. The fact that she also didn't want to sleep with him had obviously never crossed his mind. She sighed and looked down at the key in her hand. Two minutes ago, she'd felt tired and worn out, but now her fatigue was gone. In its place was an unhappy restlessness, and she suddenly hated the idea of shutting herself into the stateroom and going to bed in that claustrophobic room with its tiny porthole. What she really wanted to do, she discovered, was go up on deck, stand at the railing and watch the stars and the Grecian moon move overhead.

Impulsively, she turned in the opposite direction to David's and climbed the stairs that led to the foredeck of the ship, taking a deep breath when the cool of the night air hit her. It was refreshing after the smoky ballroom and the air-conditioned corridors. And the quiet was lovely; she had the foredeck to herself and could only faintly hear the music from the ballroom wafting in her direction.

Samantha looked over the rail and watched the water slip under the bow. Then she gazed upward towards the stars that gleamed and the bone-white crescent of the moon and felt the tension in her muscles begin to slip away. If only life could always be like this, she thought wistfully, this moment when time is suspended, when the body becomes one with the wind and the water, when the mind can freewheel in space, shedding its cares and problems and pain.

And she was so lost in her thoughts that she never heard the footstep behind her or the sudden intake of breath. She only felt the hand touch her, the warmth of the palm against her skin, the silken feel of fingers on her neck.

CHAPTER FIVE

SAMANTHA whirled around, her pulse beating wildly, screamed into the night air, tripped over her own high heel and fell directly into Josh's arms sending him staggering.

For a few seconds, they merely tried to find their breaths, then Josh demanded, 'What the hell were you trying to do? Kill me?'

Samantha stared into his face, its planes and angles emphasised by the faint rays of the moon. 'You frightened me!'

'I think that's the first time in my life I've been mistaken for a rapist!'

But now Samantha was regaining some composure. Her pulse had slowed to a less rapid rhythm and her heart, which had threatened to leap out of her throat, had subsided to its proper location in her chest.

'Well,' she said, shaking herself back to reality, 'I guess it's time to. . .'

But she never had a chance to finish what she was going to say, because his hand moved quickly t pinion her wrist and he said, 'Hear the music?'

'The music?'

'Listen.'

She obediently stood still and listened. Far away in the distance, the refrain of 'I Could Have Danced All Night' could be heard over the sound of her own breathing, the soft lapping of waves against the boat.

It echoed faintly over the water, rising into the night sky.

'It seems a shame to waste it, doesn't it?' He had turned to face her now, his shirt gleaming whitely in the moonlight, his eyes unreadable in the faint illumination.

'Waste what?'

'The song.'

'How can you waste a song?'

'Samantha, have you no imagination?'

'Now look,' she said, bristling, 'if this is to be a defamation of my character, then I would prefer it if you. . .'

'Oh, Samantha,' he said with a grin, 'has anyone ever told you that you're quite impossible?'

'Never,' she said tartly. 'In fact, I'm quite reasonable and get along with most people. I am calm and even-tempered and considered likeable by my friends and acquaintances.' She would have gone on, but now he was laughing. *Despicable man*! She really found it very difficult to tolerate him. Even when he wasn't in one of his more infuriating moods, he seemed to know precisely how to get under her skin. And he was still holding on to her wrist. 'Will you please let go of me?' she added.

'Nope,' he said. 'Even if you don't have any imagination, I do.'

'As I said,' she began hotly, 'I really don't like it when you slander my character, and furthermore. . .' Oh, she was really getting into it now! She could feel her ire rising and with it her lawyer's confrontational mentality. This was one time that Joshua Sinclair was not going to win an argument with her. 'And furthermore,' she said, drawing herself up to her full height which was woefully inadequate considering the fact that he topped her by at least six inches. 'Furthermore . . .'

His head inclined a bit. 'May I have this dance, Miss Lorimer of 93rd Street?'

And she found herself drawn into his arms as the saxophone picked up the melody, its sweet and languorous voice singing out into the dark of the night. She wanted to protest; she wanted to argue and battle and resist, but, for the first time that night, she found she had no more fight left in her. It was as if her conscious mind had yielded before the desires of her subconscious. Without thinking, she raised her hands to Josh's shoulders, while his hands fell gently to her waist. Her head tucked against his shoulder, his chin rested softly against her hair. Circling slowly, they moved closer and closer together until his breath lifted a strand of her hair, and her fingers linked together at the back of his neck.

Samantha would never be certain later just how long they had danced all by themselves, alone, on that deserted part of the ship's deck. She only knew that it did come to an end, a reluctant drawing apart, still without words, almost without breathing as if neither of them dared even to break, for one second, a magic that had been wrought out of nothing more substantial than the air around them. For a second they looked at one another, their faces shrouded by the darkness, and then his head bent, blocking out the stars and moon, creating even a deeper blackness before her. Lips brushed against hers, soft and yet masculine, firm and yet yielding when she moved her head slightly forward to capture that caress. But then his mouth was gone, and she had lifted her hand to her lips in the hopes of capturing its imprint, only to find that it, like the man, had vanished.

The island of Mykonos, Samantha discovered the
next morning, must have been the subject of every
postcard she'd ever seen of Greece. It was set like a
dazzling gem in the midst of the blue Aegean, its
town looking from a distance like a white, cubist
sculpture set against a hillside. Every small square
house was white, every wall was white, even the
stone-flagged alleys were white. Only the Byzantine
churches provided a touch of colour; their domes
were pale blue or red, dotting the monochromatic
whites like daubs of a paintbrush. Up the hill, at the
side of the town, was a row of squat windmills with
their white sides and dark, thatched roofs.

Samantha had spent most of the morning
wandering through Mykonos and peering into some
of the town's three hundred and sixty-five churches,
with their small stained glass windows and gold
icons on their altars. Old women dressed all in black
would stare at her when she first walked in and then
turn away with indifference. All the inhabitants of
tiny Mykonos seemed to be like that. The sailors on
the shore, the housewives hanging out their laundry,
the small children dashing underfoot seemed to be
completely uninterested in her or any of the other
tourists that flocked the streets, looking into
windows, wandering in and out of stores, or crowding
the beaches. It was the shopkeepers who had the
strongest investment in Mykonos' tourist trade.

Samantha glanced at the dresses pinned up to the
white walls, their gauzy skirts spread out like
butterfly wings, and the ornately decorated leather
bags hanging from outdoor racks, but she walked
quickly on. She wasn't ready to spend her drachmas
yet; she was planning on doing most of her shopping

in Athens, and besides, she had no real heart for it today. She was too tired from the day before and too confused by what had occurred the night before to feel very enthusiastic about shopping. She had gone back to the stateroom after Josh had disappeared into the dark. She'd undressed, washed off her make-up and gone to bed, lying awake for what seemed like hours, staring up at the ceiling and wondering.

She had tried to decipher the meaning of that silent dance. Was it just a stolen moment in time when two people who were essentially strangers joined under the moonlight—a pleasant but meaningless experience? Or was it something more? A statement of intention perhaps, of romantic interest, of emotions too fragile to bear the weight of words. But that seemed far too imaginative. Josh didn't like her; she didn't like him—they tended to rub each other the wrong way. Which brought her to another peculiarity of the evening. Why, she wondered, hadn't she stopped the dance from happening? All it would have taken was one negative word, one gesture of refusal, one small expression of the revulsion she should have felt. But she hadn't been revolted at all—that was the odd and damning thing. She had . . . well, she had quite enjoyed the sensation of being in Josh's arms.

Of course, she had explained to herself, it had nothing to do with the man involved. It was merely the result of an overdose of moonlight and music. Yes, she'd thought, turning over in the bed once again and plumping up her pillow for the umpteenth time, yes, of course, that's the answer—a softening of attitude brought about by a fatal combination of fatigue and the night air.

One would have thought that, once Samantha had

decided all this to her satisfaction, she would have fallen asleep with no problem at all. But sleep had remained horribly elusive, and she'd lain awake for what seemed like hours, straining to hear the sound of Josh entering the stateroom, pulling out the sofa bed, undressing and going to sleep. But the room had remained silent, with only the hum of the ship's engines filling the air, and Samantha had not been able to stop wondering where he had gone after that silent moment when his lips had met hers. He could, she had supposed as she tossed and turned, have gone back to the dance and into the arms of the lovely redhead. Or perhaps he was merely sipping at a drink at the bar or, having walked around the ship, stopped to stand at the railing, as she had done, contemplating the moonlit sea. Of course, she couldn't be sure that any of her conjectures were true, but of one thing she was absolutely positive. It was quite obvious that Josh hadn't wanted to see her again that night and was staying away from the stateroom as long as possible so that he could be sure she would be asleep when he returned.

Well, she thought, as she made her way down to the Mykonos harbour to rejoin the liner, it really doesn't matter, does it? She had no real reason to care about Josh's whereabouts, although she'd also been quite shocked to discover, the next morning, that he had come in some time during the night and had already left before she had ever risen. Not that he'd left a mess in the room; he was really quite neat, the bed had been made and rearranged as a sofa, all the clothes in his closet were neatly hung away, but the evidence that he had spent the night in the stateroom lay in his razor on the bathroom shelf and the damp towel that smelled faintly of his cologne that hung over the shower rack. Samantha could hardly believe that she'd not heard him get up and take a shower, but then she'd slept late, not rising until after ten o'clock and missing breakfast altogether. When she realised that, she'd hurriedly gathered her things together; her bag, her camera, her guide-book, pulled on a bright yellow sundress and matching sandals, run a comb through her tangle of dark curls and hurried off the ship.

But still Samantha couldn't repress the fleeting thought: how had Josh been spending the day—and with whom . . .?

CHAPTER SIX

THE NIGHT after the *Princess Marguerita* steamed out of Mykonos harbour, it was hit by a tropical storm. The warning had come during dinner, with the captain announcing that the storm would arrive but that it would be quite minor and no one was to panic. He did suggest that passengers stay in their rooms and not wander around the deck as there would be high winds and rain. The storm, he had added, was expected to blow over by morning.

Samantha went to sleep that night without once thinking about the impending gale. For one thing, it had been a beautiful clear evening with the stars out in full force and the moon beaming down. For another thing, she had enough on her mind to worry about without being concerned about the elements. She was, she knew, supposed to be finding her Greek cruise relaxing, exciting and romantic, but things were not turning out the way her grandmother had planned them. The fact was that she felt as if she were having a shipboard romance shoved down her throat, and she didn't like it all.

The problem was that the singles on the cruise had paired off almost immediately. It was as if no one had dared to remain unattached for too long for fear of being branded as a hopeless dead-loss. Marybeth and Reuben were a couple, and Marvin and Betty too seemed to have joined forces.

Josh, of course, was constantly in the company of his redhead. Samantha had seen them dancing, swimming, sightseeing, drinking and eating together. To all intents and purposes, it was a relationship that looked as solid as the rock of Gibraltar. It was funny how much the realisation of that had hurt. Seeing Josh dancing with the woman had given Samantha such a feeling of actual physical pain that, for a second, she had quite literally been bereft of breath. But of course, one doesn't die from pain like that, and she had merely shrugged it off and talked vivaciously with David and her friends. Later she had chastised herself severely for being so sentimental. Just because a man likes to dance in the moonlight and bestow fleeting kisses in the dark it does not mean that he has any permanent intentions. She had been well aware of that and really had been quite relieved that he hadn't. She didn't like him—remember? But it would appear that, in her secret heart of hearts, she had cherished some tiny, silly, romantic hope.

Ridiculous. Absolutely ridiculous.

No, Josh wasn't her problem. David was. Dear, sweet David. What on earth was she going to do about him? Samantha turned over, pulled the sheets up over her shoulders and sighed. She couldn't blame him, really she couldn't. He'd come on this trip, seeking relaxation, fun and a woman. And he was a perfectly decent, eligible man whom most women would find attractive and appealing. Except, it seemed, for Samantha. She liked him; she enjoyed dancing with him; she had a great time talking politics with him. The trouble was that she absolutely abhorred kissing him. And he wasn't going to be content with kisses for much longer. David was thirty-five, a swinging bachelor and knowledgeable about women. Most women, that was. He simply had no idea that Samantha wasn't being bowled over by his expertise in lovemaking. Take that evening, for example.

After dinner Samantha had found herself walking with him on the deck, when he had stopped her, pulled her into a corner and started to kiss her.

Samantha tried to respond, but she couldn't. There simply wasn't anything there. And she couldn't help shivering when his hand ran over the bodice of her dress, coming to rest lightly on her breast.

His head bent to kiss her again, and Samantha had put two hands on his shoulders. 'David, let's not.'

'You know, Samantha,' he had said, giving her a small, knowing smile, 'you're really different. Most of the women I know are more aggressive than men—they can't wait to hop into bed. But you're a little shy, aren't you? A little prim and old-fashioned.'

'David, it's not just a matter of being shy. You see, the chemistry can be wrong and two people just don't. . .' she couldn't quite come out and say it, so she reverted to past history, '... I had an unfortunate experience with a man that I. . .'

'Samantha,' David said soothingly, 'you don't have to explain it to me. We've all been burnt at one time or another, and if that's made you a little wary, I can understand it. But you'll see, I won't rush you, and it'll be great. Really great.'

Really great. Really disastrous. Just what was she going to do? David wasn't getting the subtle message, and Samantha shrank from the idea of blatantly coming out and telling him what she felt. The words would be ugly and painful, and she hated the idea of hurting him. He was so nice and kind and trusting. And so completely off base where she was concerned. Shy? For her whole life, no one had ever thought that Samantha was shy. Opinionated, yes. Stubborn, definitely. But shy? Never. Not even a courtroom full of judge, jury, witnesses and audience could faze her. And as for prim and old-fashioned. . . well, she was hardly that. She could be as lustful as the next woman and, if she ever met the right man, she would be just as capable of swooning with passion. She knew she could, because her dreams told her so. She sometimes had the most extraordinarily sensual dreams.

It was the memory of those dreams that finally allowed her to fall asleep, and she was caught up in one when, hours later, the impending storm broke over the *Princess Marguerita*. It came, like many semi-tropical storms, with great speed and a steadily growing ferocity. Lightning cracked open the sky with jagged bolts, followed by great threatening rolls of thunder. Winds whipped and whirled, first driving the clouds into a roiling turbulence and then sweeping the water before it so that the calm of the Mediterranean gave way to white-capped waves that crashed against the sides of the ship.

Samantha was quite oblivious to the winds, the rocking or the rain that battered against the small porthole by her head. She was sleeping deeply, caught up in the entangling fascination of a dream. It was an odd dream: in it, she was naked and wrapped up in a cocoon with a naked man. His body against hers was warm and hot; he had dark, wavy hair, wide-set dark eyes and he looked like. . .

'*Josh*!'

The scream was almost simultaneous with the huge crack of thunder that made her sit up straight in bed, eyes wide open, her heart beating madly in her chest, her hands pressed trembling to the bodice of her nightgown. Her sheets had fallen to the floor, and her bed was moving, sliding this way and that. In fact, the room itself seemed to be moving as the ship rose and then fell, twisted and then slid to one side.

There was a sudden flash of lightning as the bedroom door banged open and, for a milli-second, Samantha had a glimpse of Josh in the doorway. The light, eerie and white, revealed a man who was hastily tying a bathrobe around his waist, dark hair tousled, dark eyes seeking her as blackness closed around them once again.

'Samantha! Samantha, are you okay?'

She called out to him, but there was a heavy roll of thunder, a crashing boom that drowned out her voice. And beneath the ferocity of the storm were other sounds, ones that made her freeze. There was a crash against the far wall of the room, a muttered curse, another crash closer to her and then a cry of pain. Then, as the thunder died away, there was a frightening silence.

'Oh, my God,' Samantha whispered to herself. She scrambled off the bed, groped past her bedside-table and then had to grab on to a chair to keep herself upright as the *Princess Marguerita* slid sideways again.

'Josh!' she called out. 'Josh, where are you?'

There was no answer except the banging of her bedroom door as it swayed back and forth with the motion of the boat. Samantha crawled on her hands and knees towards the door, thinking that perhaps he had been hit by it, perhaps. . . her hand touched warm, hard flesh. Experimentally, she ran her fingers along the flesh, feeling the crisp hair, the curve of muscle, the bone of a. . . kneecap.

'Josh? Josh, are you all right?' she whispered as her hands quickly moved up his prone body, nervously touching here and there, over the hem of his terry-cloth robe, its knotted tie, a lapel. She tried hard to ignore the other messages her hands were receiving: messages about the hardness and softness of a man, about the planes and angles that made a man's body so different from a woman's. Instead she concentrated on getting to his head. He was twisted on his side with one arm flung upwards, the other lying palm down to the ground. She found a shoulder, his neck, the curve of his jaw and an ear.

'Josh,' she whispered urgently. 'Can you hear me?'

But his silence was ominous, and she grew even more frightened than she already was.

'Oh, Josh,' she said desperately. 'Please, please wake up!'

She turned him over, slowly, gently, allowing the heavy weight of him to fall on her bent legs. Then she leaned over him once again, her hands touching his face. 'Wake up, come on now, wake up!' The words repeated themselves over and over again, a whispered litany of pleading and prayer. She wrapped her arms around him, lay across him, unaware of the softness of her breasts flattening against his arm or the way her leg entwined around his. 'Please, please. Wake up! Come on, wake up!' And all around her, the storm raged unabated, the ship rocking, rain driving hard and fast against the porthole's glass window.

Then Samantha felt Josh shaking beneath her, his shoulders moving, the muscles of his stomach clenching and unclenching. She sat up quickly and grabbed his shoulders. 'Josh?' she said tentatively. 'Are you all right?' He was making an odd, horrible

sound—like someone who was trying to breathe—
no, like someone who could breathe but was choking
or strangling or. . . was he *crying*? Samantha's heart
did a peculiar flip-flop in her chest. 'Josh?'

Lightning flared again, a huge, jagged spear that
rent the sky in two, angling from one corner of the
firmament to another, piercing the clouds, striking
deep into the sea. It lit up the whole world, revealing
the black depths of the clouds, the arcing waves, the
water-washed deck of the *Princess Marguerita*.
Finally there was a silence, not a complete silence as
the rain still beat against the window and the boat
still shuddered and the bedroom door still smacked
against the wall, but the sort of silence that occurs
when a man and a woman are in the process of con-
frontation.

Samantha broke it. 'You louse!' she hissed. 'You
lousy cad! You bastard!'

And her hands were now clenched together, not
out of fear for her safety or his life, but because she
was afraid that if she let them go, they would wrap
themselves around Josh's neck and squeeze hard.

'Samantha,' he said.

She would have liked to sink below the ground,
disappear into some forgiving oblivion, be obliter-
ated by some obliging nuclear blast. Anything was
better than sitting there, cringing with the knowledge
of how she had acted, of what she must have sounded
like, of the sentimental idiot she had been. She had
pleaded with him to be alive, throwing herself over
him, practically kissing him in her desperation to
bring him back to consciousness. And all the
while. . . She rocked back on her heels and brought
her clenched fists up to her burning cheeks. . . all the
while, he'd been wide awake and trying hard not to

laugh. Because that was what she had seen, when the lightning had illuminated the room. His grin. His damned lazy grin!

'I hate you,' she added flatly.

'Come here,' he said.

'You must be joking!'

'I want to talk to you,' he insisted.

'Talk to me! Why didn't you talk to me five minutes ago when I was begging you to? Well, I suppose it was more fun to let me think you were dying. I'll bet you got a hell of a good charge out of that!'

'Samantha.'

'. . . and I just love being made a fool of. It's so. . . so. . .'

'Hush, Sam.' And suddenly she was being pulled down to the floor and brought into his arms. She struggled against him, but he was far stronger than she was. Besides, it was obvious that the boat itself was against her. Each time she did manage to push herself away, a sudden lurch of the *Princess Marguerita* sent her right back into Josh's embrace. Finally, she gave up and lay rigid in his arms. He brought her head on to his shoulder and stroked the hair that curled at her temple. 'Don't be angry,' he said softly.

'I am not *angry*,' Samantha said hotly. 'I'm furious!'

'And I do appreciate what you were doing.'

'Well, who *wouldn't*? What man wouldn't appreciate having a half-naked woman slobbering all over him?'

'You weren't slobbering.'

'Oh, what's the difference?' Samantha snapped in disgust. She refused to soften; she didn't care one bit about the effort he was taking to make her feel better. She didn't care about the gentle fingers at her temple or the strong arm around her shoulders.

'I did manage to knock myself out, you know. Hit my head against something.' His hand left her hair and went to touch his own head. 'Ouch—it's starting to swell.'

'I'm sure the nurse will be delighted to look at it,' Samantha said coldly. Frankly, she hoped he'd have the world's largest goose egg and mankind's worst headache.

His fingers went back to tangling themselves in her hair. 'But then I came to and you were on top of me and. . . well, hell's bells, I never wanted it to come to an end.'

'Just don't get any fancy ideas,' Samantha said coldly. 'Now that I know you're alive, I couldn't care less.'

'You don't mean that, Sam.'

'Samantha—and yes, I do. Now look, if you're finished having this little talk why don't you just let me go and we can get some sleep.'

'Sleep?' he asked. 'In this storm? You're the one who woke up—remember?'

Another crash of thunder broke over them. 'I can't imagine what woke me up,' she said untruthfully, 'and frankly, I'm exhausted and would like to. . .'

'Besides, I like calling you Sam. Samantha is too. . . mm, abstract.'

'Abstract? What are you talking about?'

'Sam sounds cuddly.'

'You've got the wrong woman, then,' she said firmly. 'I am not the cuddly type.'

'That's funny,' he said. 'You sure feel like one.'

Samantha discovered that she'd relaxed in his arms. Her body had moved closer to his, her head was resting against his arm, her leg touched his at thigh, knee and ankle. Quickly, she made herself rigid again and tried to push herself away from him. 'Let me go!'

'I'd like to conduct a little test.'

She despairingly wondered why every conversation that she had with Josh always took such odd directions.

'What sort of a test?' she said with resignation.

It was quite possible that Josh was once again grinning into the darkness, but his voice didn't give it away. 'A small test that won't take but a moment of your time. Nothing dramatic.'

'What does it involve?' she asked suspiciously.

'Just you and me. Look,' he said, 'here's how it goes. I turn slightly this way.' He moved his body so that her head was off his shoulder and lying on his upper arm, his torso was turned to her, and the hand that had been stroking her hair had now moved down to her waist. 'And you move slightly that way.' That hand pulled her closer to him. 'And then I go like this.'

Of course, Samantha was no fool. She'd known perfectly well what Josh was up to, and she now knew perfectly well what she would do—slap him across the face, get out of his arms, tell him where to get off and never to come back. But she didn't do any of those perfectly logical things. The moment seemed to conspire against all her sane and logical conclusions. The carpet was thick and plush beneath her, the room was so dark that she couldn't have seen her hand in front of her face, and the storm raged futilely outside the window. It was warm and safe and cosy in Josh's arms, and she discovered that she really didn't want to get up and go back to her bed. What she really wanted was a return to her dream: the dream of the silk cocoon. It was the memory of that dream that made her body curve against his, her face to tilt up to his, her lips to meet his.

She responded in a way she had not responded with any other man of her intimate acquaintance. A warmth flooded through her; her body seemed to melt against his, every nerve in her skin aching for the touch of his skin. Her fingers tangled in his hair; her breasts filled and swelled beneath the pressure of his chest. For several wild and uninhibited moments, she completely forgot who—she was kissing, whose body lay entwined with hers, whose mouth played havoc with her emotions. Her hand moved from his hair to his bathrobe and slipped beneath it to stroke the sleek warmth of his shoulder. His hand left her waist, moving to her hip below the rucked-up hem of her nightgown, and she moaned when his fingers travelled, slowly, teasingly, erotically, to the soft curve between her legs.

It was quite possible that they would have actually made love that night, lying on the carpeted floor of that darkened room, rocked by the movement of the boat. They had, somehow, become one with the storm, their passions rising, their motions frantic as they sought to come together, Josh's bathrobe slipped off, her nightgown pulled up over her head. There was a rightness to the feel of their bodies together that neither of them had expected, but that neither of them could deny. It was elemental, primal, overwhelming. It ripped apart logic, rationality and common sense. It reduced Samantha to nothing more than a woman responding to a man, to an urgent need to be filled, to an aching desire for satiation. Everything else in her had fled before the driving heat of that passion.

They came so close to actual union that it was only the shock of ice-cold water that made them stop. The porthole catch had broken, the window sprang open and rain sprayed over them. Samantha gasped, broke out of Josh's embrace and then shivered as the cold air hit her heated, bare skin. Realising how truly naked she was, she quickly pulled down her nightgown. There was a banging of the window as Josh got up and closed it, a cessation of wind and rain and then the faint rumble of thunder off in the distance. The *Princess Marguerita*, Samantha realised, was no longer rocking about so wildly and her room had stabilised so that she could now stand up, move about, find the light switch that turned on the wall lamp by her bed.

The intensity of illumination startled both of them, and Samantha quickly turned around so that she could no longer see Josh's aroused nudity. 'Please go,' she said, her voice husky as if she had not used it for hours.

'Sam.'

'No.' She shrugged away the hand he had put on her shoulder.

'Sam, I'm sorry.'

'I'll bet you are!'

'I didn't intend for things to go that far.'

'Get out!'

He turned her slowly around, and she stood there with her eyes closed, her face pink and flushed beneath the tumble of her dark hair, her mouth swollen and tremulous. 'It was a mistake,' he said. 'Just a mistake. Sam, look at me.'

'No!'

'I'm decent now—you don't have to be afraid to look.'

'Go away!'

His hands tightened on her shoulders and she could feel his frustration in them, but she wasn't going to give in this time or be sweet-talked into something she didn't want to do. Besides, another thought had come to her, one that made her stiffen even further and kept her eyes clamped shut. *No*, she said to herself, *no, it can't be true.*

He sighed. 'Would it make you feel any better if I told you that I don't understand how it happened either?'

But Samantha was barely listening to him. Instead her brain was reeling with the thought of it. Impossible. *Impossible!* Margaret had said she would cancel the Fantasy Unlimited contract. Cassie had promised that she would see it was done. But suppose she hadn't? Suppose Josh were the hired man? *No, it simply couldn't be true.*

'Will you let me apologise?'

Suppose Margaret had arranged for Samantha to share a room with Josh? *But he hadn't liked the arrangement any more than she had.* But he hadn't been quite as upset by it, had he? Besides, her grandmother knew her very well. Just suppose she'd given Josh instructions not to be too forward, too romantic all at once. That would have aroused Samantha's suspicions, so Josh had basically ignored her, taken up with another woman and had just bided his time until. . . *until what? A storm came along? Come on, Samantha, don't be ridiculous. Margaret may be a bit crazy, but she isn't capable of creating a storm over the Mediterranean.*

'Samantha, I'm going to go now.' Josh's fingers tightened convulsively on her shoulders. 'Damn it, are you listening?'

Her eyes opened and she stared straight at him. There was no amusement at all in his dark eyes. There was anger present, but also something else that she couldn't decipher. A remnant of passion, perhaps? A macho satisfaction that he hadn't wanted to admit to? Samantha had no way of reading Josh's mood. His face was devoid of expression, and the tone of his voice was cool.

'Yes,' she said. 'You're going.'

His hands dropped from her shoulders. 'You'll be able to sleep now?'

'Yes, I'm. . . I'm sorry about calling you before. I shouldn't have.'

'It was a bad storm.'

They were both so polite that a stranger would never have guessed that ten minutes before they'd been entangled in an erotic, intimate embrace.

'Yes, it was.'

'Goodnight, then.'

'Goodnight,' said Samantha, her voice equally non-committal, distant and cool as she watched Josh walk out of the bedroom door.

It wasn't until the door was firmly closed behind him, and she was absolutely positive that he wouldn't come back, that Samantha finally allowed her rigidity to give way to despair and exhaustion. With a moan of misery, she slumped down on the edge of the bed and put her head into her hands, covering her face, her eyes, trying hard to obliterate the images in her mind. But certain pictures would not go away; a vision of her lying across Josh's body, of her enfolded in his arms, of their legs twisted together. And she shuddered slightly as his touch came back to her, the warmth of his mouth, the feel of his hard body beneath her hands.

Samantha reached up, switched off the light and crawled back into bed, pulling up the sheets that had fallen to one side. She'd try to sleep now, she thought as she closed her eyes and let her head fall on the pillow. She'd sleep, and when she woke up tomorrow, the whole night would feel as if it were a dream, a wisp, an illusion. Like all her dreams, it would fade in the bright light of day, its power waning, its colours shading off into sepia tones as it disappeared into the air. And then, in the way of dreams, it would remain as a shadow, just out of sight, elusive as a will-o'-the-wisp, its events forgotten for all time.

CHAPTER SEVEN

THE NEXT morning, before the ship docked at the island of Rhodes, ninety-nine per cent of all the conversation on board the *Princess Marguerita* was about the storm the night before.

But there was one conversation that was taking place on the deck of the ship that had nothing to do with the storm. Marybeth and David were sitting in deck chairs, morosely watching the reflection of the sun glitter on the now tranquil Mediterranean.

'I can't seem to get past first base with Samantha,' David was confessing.

Marybeth sat up in her chair. If there was one thing she liked almost as much as flirting, it was giving advice to the lovelorn. 'Are you going about it the right way?' she asked him.

'I thought I was. I thought she liked me.'

'Why, David, she does. You're probably just coming on too strong for her!'

'And what about that guy she shares a room with?'

'Oh, him,' said Marybeth. 'You don't have to worry about him.'

'You're sure?'

'Absolutely. She can't stand the sight of him, that's what she told me. No, all you have to do, David, is sweep her off her feet. Sincerity is the thing, honest-to-goodness romantic sincerity.'

'Like flowers?'

'Well,' mused Marybeth, 'flowers sure don't hurt. Right, here's what I think you should do.'

Within seconds, they were far too deep into a whispering, conspiratorial discussion to notice when a tall, dark figure rose up from a deck chair that had been placed behind them. As their heads bent closer together, they missed the appraising glance that he gave them. And finally, when they were finished talking and had decided it was time to go, they left without the slightest inkling that anyone had overheard their conversation, or that their words had triggered an unexpected line of thought, or that what they had said would alter the course of events to the point that nothing would be as it seemed. Left would be right, up would be down, black would be white and love, unmeasurable and elusive, would play the masquerade, a harlequin, a jester, its features and motives hidden until that moment when it would reveal itself as the holder of hearts, hearts dangling from glowing red and blue ribbons, tangled together, knotted and bow-tied, caught for ever in that sweet and richly-coloured web.

Samantha had seen every tourist attraction that Rhodes had to offer in the space of one action-packed morning. Her group, led by a knowledgeable tour guide, went into the walled Old Town and saw Greek ruins, Roman statues, medieval monuments and Turkish mosques, the evidence of hundreds of years of domination by many different masters. They absorbed the history of the island, a history primarily made up, as far as Samantha could tell, by one battle after another in which the ancient Rhodians were forced to take sides, not always the right one. She tried so hard to imagine the island as it must have once been with invaders strutting across the landscape, but it was hard to envisage a para-military state when confronted with modern Rhodes, a tourist town far larger than Mykonos with bustling, tree-lined streets lined with shops and restaurants.

'And, of course, what made Rhodes so famous in antiquity was the Colossus, a thirty-two-metre-high sculpture of a man who stood astride the harbour so that ships could sail between his legs. He was considered one of the Seven Wonders of the Ancient World.' The tour guide paused, glanced at the circle of people in front of her to make sure they had all got the import of her statement, and then she went on, 'But in 225 BC there was an earthquake that caused it to crumble.'

A woman standing near Samantha looked alarmed. 'Does Greece have a lot of earthquakes?' she asked.

As the tour guide went on to reassure her flock that no, there were very few earthquakes in Greece, Samantha decided that she'd had enough. She slipped away from the group, hailed a taxi whose driver spoke pidgin English and went back to the area around Mandraki Harbour where the large hotels were situated and where the *Princess Marguerita* was docked. It was another beautiful day. The storm had cleared away whatever clouds had hung over the horizon and the sky was incredibly blue. Even though it was still mid-morning, sun-worshippers were already lying prone on the beach, and amorous couples strolled hand in hand along the water's edge.

Samantha determinedly looked away from them and hurried back to the boat. She had no intention of thinking about anything that had to do with love or lovemaking. She had managed to keep her mind off the subject ever since leaving the ship that morning, and the measure of her success was that she hadn't thought about Josh for at least an hour. Of course, it hadn't been easy to ignore him when she had woken up. For the first time since the cruise began, they had actually been in the stateroom together before breakfast. Prior to that Josh had always been gone before she had got up.

Politeness had been the order of the morning. Considering the size of the stateroom and the fact that they had to share one bathroom, the way they had managed to avoid one another had been nothing short of miraculous. They had tiptoed around, not made eye contact and had exchanged short, courteous sentences.

Samantha winced as she remembered it all. There couldn't have been two people more embarrassed or more uncomfortable with one another than her and Joshua Sinclair. Of course, she was glad that Josh hadn't wanted to bring up the subject of their lovemaking any more than she had. His actions just went to prove what she had thought all along—that the episode had been purely accidental and that he'd regretted it just as much as she had. And, if she had had even the slightest shred of suspicion left that Josh was part of Margaret's Fantasy Unlimited scheme, it was swept away by his behaviour that morning. A hired escort, Samantha thought, would have acted differently. He would have had flowers delivered to her that morning while she was still in bed. No, not a large bunch of ostentatious chrysanthemums or marigolds, but one flower—a single, subtle rose. Samantha could see it: the long-stemmed red rose, lying on a tray, accompanied by a small envelope. She would have opened the envelope and taken out the small white card with its message in a decisive script. He would, of course, be begging for her forgiveness.

PLAY THE "LUCKY 7" SLOT MACHINE GAME !

AND YOU COULD GET FREE BOOKS, A FREE UMBRELLA AND A SURPRISE GIFT!

NO COST! NO OBLIGATION!
NO PURCHASE NECESSARY!

PLAY "LUCKY 7"
AND GET AS MANY AS SIX FREE GIFTS...

HOW TO PLAY:

1. With a coin, carefully scratch off the three silver boxes at the right. This makes you eligible to receive one or more free books, and possibly other gifts, depending on what is revealed beneath the scratch-off area.

2. You'll receive brand-new Harlequin Presents® novels, never before published. When you return this card, we'll send you the books and gifts you qualify for *absolutely free!*

3. And, a month later, we'll send you 8 additional novels to read and enjoy. If you decide to keep them, you'll pay only $1.99 per book, a savings of 26¢ per book. And $1.99 per book is all you pay. There is no charge for shipping and handling. There are no hidden extras.

4. We'll also send you additional free gifts from time to time, as well as our newsletter.

5. You must be completely satisfied, or you may return a shipment of books and cancel at any time.

FOLDING UMBRELLA FREE

This bright burgundy umbrella is made of durable nylon. It folds to a compact 15″ to fit into your bag or briefcase. And it could be YOURS FREE when you play "LUCKY 7."

PLAY "LUCKY 7"

*Just scratch off the three silver boxes.
Then check below to see which gifts you get.*

YES! I have scratched off the silver boxes. Please send me all the gifts for which I qualify. I understand I am under no obligation to purchase any books, as explained on the opposite page.

108 CIP CAMK

_____

NAME

_____

ADDRESS   APT..

_____

CITY   STATE   ZIP

 WORTH FOUR FREE BOOKS, FREE UMBRELLA AND FREE SURPRISE GIFT

 WORTH FOUR FREE BOOKS AND FREE UMBRELLA

 WORTH FOUR FREE BOOKS

 WORTH TWO FREE BOOKS

NO POSTAGE
NECESSARY
IF MAILED
IN THE
UNITED STATES

BUSINESS REPLY CARD

First Class   Permit No. 717   Buffalo, NY

Postage will be paid by addressee

Harlequin Reader Service ®
901 Fuhrmann Blvd.
P.O. Box 1394
Buffalo, NY 14240-9963

'Samantha darling. . .' No, perhaps the rose would come without any message at all, its mere presence letting her know. . .

As she hurried up the gangplank of the *Princess Marguerita*, Samantha wondered if she weren't going just a little bit crazy. Imagine falling for such a misty, romantic cliché!

She decided to take herself off for a sunbathing session, with a good book to take her mind off its wandering. But it was not to be.

'Excuse me,' a soft voice said as she reached the sun-deck. 'Could I speak to you for a moment?'

She turned to face a woman who was taller than she was, elegant in a silky blue lounging outfit, whose nails were manicured to a high scarlet sheen, whose eyes were an emerald green and whose coiled hair held all the colours of firelight. She was the kind of woman who made other women, Samantha included, feel awkward, plain and undesirable.

'We haven't been introduced,' the soft voice went on, 'but I know who you are, so I hope you don't mind this intrusion.'

Samantha knew who she was, too. She'd seen her often enough, leaning towards Josh, talking to him, smiling at him, dancing with him. Samantha had also developed an irrational and intense dislike of her. There was no reason on earth, she had told herself with a lawyerlike logic, that she should care one way or the other about a woman she didn't know. But for some reason the antagonism had remained and, despite all her efforts to root it out of her system, it was intact, healthy and thriving with a real vengeance.

Now it made her voice cool and polite. 'No,' she said, 'not at all.'

The other woman waved her scarlet-tipped hand at a couple of sun-loungers in a quiet corner. 'We could sit over here.'

'Certainly.'

They sat down, and the other woman cleared her throat. 'My name is Helen, by the way. Helen Moore.'

'Samantha Lorimer.'

'Yes, Josh told me. You're sharing a room with him, by mistake, he said. A computer error.'

Did she doubt it? Samantha wondered. There was something in her voice that suggested that Helen Moore wasn't quite sure that Josh had been telling her the truth. 'Yes,' she said, and wondered whether it was relief or not that she saw flashing in those green eyes.

'It's really quite ridiculous, isn't it?'

'Yes,' said Samantha.

'You didn't know one another before the cruise, did you?'

Interesting and even more interesting. Samantha was definitely beginning to wonder why Helen Moore was so intent on nailing down the facts.

'No,' she said, 'we didn't.'

Helen's laugh was silvery, graceful and quite careless. 'You know, Josh and I have got quite close.'

Close. What exactly did she mean by—close? Did it have a definition that went beyond what one would find in a dictionary?

'How nice—for you.'

'And I hadn't really expected to meet anyone like him on this cruise. In fact, I wasn't going to come, but my family insisted.' Helen gave Samantha a brave smile. 'I was widowed, you see, last year.'

'Oh, I'm sorry to hear that.'

'Of course, my husband was much older than I was. It was a heart attack—not unexpected, he'd been having troubles.' Samantha could see it all; the doting older husband, the young glamorous redhead who was now the rich and not-so-grieving widow. 'But life does go on, doesn't it?'

'Oh, yes,' Samantha agreed. 'It does.'

'And one can't mourn for ever.'

'No, I can see that.' But what she couldn't quite see was where this peculiar conversation was going or what Helen Moore wanted out of her.

'So, having Josh show up in my life, at this point, is very important to me. You can understand that, can't you?'

Samantha was mystified. 'Yes.'

'And it's important to Josh as well. He's just coming out of a very intense love affair.'

Samantha blinked. 'He is?'

'Oh, yes. It's been a very difficult time for him. He's very vulnerable right now.'

Samantha blinked again.

'He hasn't mentioned that to you?'

Samantha cleared her throat. 'Josh and I don't confide in one another. We're just room-mates.'

'Well, you know, I wondered if you felt differently about him.'

'Differently?' Samantha echoed sharply. 'In what way?'

'He's a very attractive man.'

Well, here it was. Out in the open. Samantha suddenly understood what this conversation was all about. Helen had first verified her facts, then she had presented her claim to Josh, defined her territory and was now in the process of keeping any invaders at bay. The fact that she had done all this in a roundabout fashion that would have done credit to the most wily legal mind almost commanded Samantha's grudging admiration. And Helen had also managed to discover, in a very short time, that she had no real competition in Samantha. She had done this very simply—by making Samantha admit that she hadn't known about Josh's past love affair.

Samantha had an almost overwhelming urge to deflate the other woman's smug belief that she had Josh sewed up tight. 'Actually,' she would have liked to say, 'he is very attractive—so attractive that we almost made love last night.' But she didn't say it, because the lovemaking, as she well knew, meant absolutely nothing.

'No,' she said, 'I don't feel differently about him. As I told you, we're just accidental room-mates.'

Helen stood up in a graceful, lithe gesture. 'I thought it best to be frank,' she said. 'I didn't want any misunderstandings or complications. It's nice when everything is kept simple, don't you think?'

Samantha stood up, too. 'Absolutely,' she agreed.

'And of course, you seem to have your own escort anyway.'

'My own escort?'

'The young man with the brown hair.'

Samantha opened her mouth to deny it, but there seemed no point in belabouring the issue to someone as inconsequential as Helen Moore, and all she said was, 'Oh, yes. David.'

But Helen didn't seem to notice Samantha's lack of enthusiasm. She merely smiled her glittering, beautiful smile and said, 'See you, then.'

'See you,' Samantha echoed as the other woman left.

As she walked down from the sun-deck and headed towards her stateroom, she tried hard not to let a pervasive depression settle over her. It wasn't pleasant being warned off a man by a woman as calculating and as aggressive as Helen Moore. Samantha couldn't help wondering why Helen had bothered to approach her in the first place. It was, she supposed, quite possible that Helen had developed suspicions all on her own. She was certainly the jealous type. But it was also quite possible that Josh had said something or inadvertently dropped a hint that had led Helen to the belief that there was more to the room-mate situation than met the eye.

Well, Samantha thought with a supreme attempt at shrugging off the feeling of depression, this would all be very fascinating and certainly fodder for a love advice column if she had any designs on Josh herself. But, since she didn't, it was strictly trivia.

'Miss Lorimer! Miss Lorimer!' It was the purser, hurrying after her. 'I'm so glad I found you.'

'I'm sorry,' said Samantha, stopping in the narrow corridor, 'I didn't know you were looking for me.'

He came to a breathless stop. 'We had a passenger disembark this morning, leaving a stateroom free.'

'Oh,' said Samantha, 'does that mean. . .?'

The purser was now beaming at her. 'So you and Mr Sinclair no longer have to share a room. I can't tell you how pleased I am that it's all turned out so well. As I was saying to Mr Sinclair, these things do happen, but it's such a pleasure when people can be accommodated.'

'Oh, then Mr Sinclair knows about it?'

'Mr Sinclair moved out this morning, Miss Lorimer. Isn't that nice?'

'Very.'

'And I have the extra key for you in my office.'

'Fine.'

'And I hope you enjoy the rest of the cruise.'

'Yes, I'm sure I will.'

Well, there, that was settled, Samantha said to herself as she said goodbye to the purser and walked on. She'd have her living room, bedroom and bathroom to herself. No more shaving cream by the sink or ties hanging from her closet. No more awkward goodbyes in the morning and embarrassing encounters during the night. Yes, she was quite relieved, she told herself as she arrived at her stateroom door and pulled the key out of her bag.

And the best part was, she thought as she opened the stateroom door and walked in, that she would no longer have to see Josh. Since she didn't sit with him during meals and no longer shared a room with him, there was no reason why their paths would have to cross except in the most casual way. In fact, on a ship as large as the *Princess Marguerita*, it was quite possible that she might not see Josh again for the rest of the trip. That was a satisfying thought, wasn't it? For once in her life, things were looking up.

Yes, everything was now arranged to her utmost satisfaction, which was why she should be elated, ecstatic and ebullient. She should be overjoyed that she had Josh out of her room and her life. She should be just thrilled to pieces that she was back on her own.

So why wasn't she?

Samantha didn't know the answer to that question, so she strode angrily over to the bedroom door and flung it open. Instead of being happy, she felt miserable. Instead of luxuriating in her privacy, she felt lonely. Instead of feeling content, she felt restless and irritable. It was as if, by leaving, Josh had unlocked a Pandora's box in Samantha that she hadn't known existed, letting loose a whole set of unwanted and unexpected and definitely unappealing emotions. And once let out, they raced around inside her, raising such a cacophony of discordant sounds and feelings that the only thing she wanted to do was throw herself head first on the bed and bury her face in her arms.

And she would have done just that if the sight of her neat and tidy bed had not brought her up short, causing her to stop in her tracks and stand rooted to the carpet. What lay so innocently across the gold counterpane was something quite inoffensive by most people's standards. In fact, in the eyes of many, the item in question would be considered as part of a pleasing, exciting and romantic gesture. But Samantha couldn't feel any of those things. She had the horrible feeling that her mind had somehow been plundered, exposed, laid bare, its silly thoughts and absurd fantasies stripped and revealed for all to see.

Because, on the bed, was a rose. A long-stemmed scarlet rose. A rose whose velvety petals had opened in a lush, blossoming splendour and whose delicate fragrance filled the air. One lovely, subtle rose.

CHAPTER EIGHT

SAMANTHA had picked up the rose and was staring at it when she was startled by a knock on the stateroom door. Her first and wildest thought was that Josh was there, wanting to find out her reaction to the rose. Her second thought was that she was entirely too fanciful and that it was probably the steward with a new set of towels. She walked through the sitting room, dropping the rose on the table, and opened the door.

Marybeth stood there. 'Is Josh here?'

'No, he moved out today.'

'Mind if I come in?'

'Of course not.'

Marybeth limped through the door, flopped down in the chair nearest the door and then stared at her legs, which were stuck out before her.

'My feet,' she said, 'are killing me.'

Samantha closed the door. 'What have you been doing?'

'Jogging—with Reuben. I guess I need to have my head examined.' Marybeth threw her head back in weariness. 'Honeybunch, could I impose on you for a little bit of something to drink?'

'Sure.' Samantha went to the small cupboard that held a tiny bar and refrigerator. 'Alcoholic or non-alcoholic?'

'Bourbon, if there is any.'

Samantha found a tiny bottle of Southern Comfort. 'On the rocks?'

'Straight—heavens, if my mother could hear me, she'd have three heart attacks! She thinks women should stick to mint juleps.'

'Here you are,' said Samantha, passing on the drink, than sitting down on the sofa.

'I really don't believe in drinking before the sun's over the yardarm, but there are times and circumstances. . .' Marybeth said ominously, giving Samantha a meaningful glance over the edge of her glass. 'Well, here's to nothing.' She took a sip of her Bourbon and then noticed the rose on the table between them. 'Why, isn't this nice,' she added, picking it up. 'Who sent you roses?'

'*A* rose,' Samantha corrected, 'and I don't know who it was. It was here without a note.'

Marybeth immediately perked up. 'I just love a man who's mysterious, don't you?'

'Only when I know who he is,' Samantha said drily.

'Well, who do you think sent it?'

'I. . . Josh, I suppose.'

Marybeth's blue eyes widened. 'Why on earth would Josh send you a rose? I thought you two didn't get along.'

Samantha cleared her throat. 'Well, we don't exactly.'

'And besides, he's hooked up with that redhead. She moved in so fast that no one else had a chance.' Marybeth gave a dramatic sigh. 'I tried, you know.'

'I. . . I thought Josh might have sent the rose, because we shared. . .' Samantha paused and then said delicately, 'a room.'

Marybeth didn't notice her hesitation. 'So?' she asked.

'Well, he might have wanted to say "thank you",' Samantha replied hesitantly, 'or something like that.'

'But one single rose. It says more than that.'

'It does?'

'Absolutely,' said Marybeth with conviction. 'Why, one rose is so understated and so delicate a touch that no man would send it just because he shared a room with a woman. No, I don't see that at all.'

'You don't?'

'Heavens, no. Now, listen to me, Samantha, the man who sent you that rose is absolutely nuts about you.'

Samantha stared at the rose that Marybeth was twirling in her fingers. 'Then who sent it to me?' she asked.

'You mean you don't know?'

'No.'

'Samantha, you aren't seeing the forest for the trees! Why, it's David, of course.'

'David!'

'Who else?'

Samantha tried to imagine David sending her that rose and failed. She could see him sending her a dozen roses; she could see them arriving with a carefully penned love note. What she could not envisage was David having enough imagination to send a single rose without a message. He was far too careful for that, and far too determined to let Samantha know exactly what he wanted. He had intelligence, a sense of humour, and a fair amount of machismo, but he didn't have subtlety. None at all.

'I don't think David sent that rose,' she said.

'He's crazy about you.'

'He doesn't. . .' Samantha tried to find a word that would describe how she felt about David. 'He isn't poetic enough.'

'You could do a lot worse than David, honeychile. Oh, I'll admit that he isn't the most exciting man around, but he's kind and considerate and he wants you. That's a lot more than you can say about any other man on this boat. If it were me, I'd snap him up so fast your head would be spinning right into tomorrow.' Marybeth gave another sigh. 'Instead, I have to put up with Reuben, who just blows hot and cold. You know what I'd like to do with that man? I'd like to. . .'

But Samantha never got a chance to find out what Marybeth would do if she ever got her hands on an elusive Reuben. There was a knock at the door, and this time it was the steward, armed with a new set of towels, a change of linen, and refills for her drinks cabinet.

Marybeth stood up, stretched and yawned. 'I'd better get ready for dinner,' she said. 'Are you going to the casino tonight?'

'The casino?' queried Samantha.

'At the Hotel Athena. They're waiving entrance fees for passengers of the *Princess Marguerita*.'

'I guess I'll go,' said Samantha.

'See you later, then,' Marybeth said as she walked towards the door. 'And thanks for the Bourbon.'

'It was a pleasure.'

'And you think about that rose some more. I really *do* think David sent it.'

Samantha wasn't quite sure what exactly it was about Marybeth that aroused her suspicions. It might have been that last little bit of persuasion or the tone of her voice or a strange expression in her wide blue eyes. Whatever it was, it was enough for her to ask slowly, 'Did you suggest to David that he send me a rose?'

Marybeth turned. 'Why, Samantha, whatever gave you that idea?'

'Marybeth,' Samantha said ominously, 'did you?'

'Cross my heart,' said Marybeth in a solemn voice, making a crossing gesture over her T-shirted chest, 'I never did.' And then with a quick little wave and a hurried step out of the door, she added, 'See you later.'

Samantha wished she could have put Marybeth up in the witness box and have her swear on the Bible that she was telling the whole truth and nothing but the truth, because she knew without a doubt that the girl was up to something that was not quite kosher. She had questioned too many witnesses not to have an instinct when someone was lying or half-lying or only telling a part of the truth. Still, she thought, there was another way of getting to the bottom of the matter, and she turned to the steward who was putting the refills of drinks in her cabinet.

'Did you deliver a rose here?' she asked.

'Yes, ma'am, I did.'

'Who sent it?'

'It just came down from the flower shop.'

She didn't want to ask, but she had to. 'With instructions to put it on the bed?'

If the steward thought there was anything unusual in delivering flowers to a lady's boudoir and laying them across something so suggestive of sexual excess as a bed, he gave no sign of it. 'Yes,' he said solemnly, 'those were the instructions.'

But a phone call later to the flower shop didn't clear up the ambiguities. The proprietress couldn't give Samantha any information because she'd only just come on duty and, as for the sales clerk earlier—well, she had to apologise, but that was her sister who lived on Rhodes and had come aboard just for the morning so that the proprietress could visit her sick mother. And no, the flower hadn't been put on anyone's room bill. The sales slip showed that the customer had paid cash. She was terribly sorry if there was some mix-up, and she could get hold of her sister the next day if it was absolutely necessary and. . .

'No,' said Samantha, 'it doesn't matter all that much. I was just curious. Thanks anyway.'

'*Kali andamosi.*'

'Goodbye.'

As she put the telephone receiver down in its cradle, Samantha realised that she was now left with one item of incriminating evidence, no witnesses, an unknown motive and possibly a secret admirer. She picked up the rose that Marybeth had dropped on the table and looked at it for a long time as if the curved scarlet petals, the drooping stamens, the delicate gold beads of pollen could answer all the questions for her. Then, with a sigh, she put it down and began to dress for the evening.

But Samantha changed her mind and never did go to the casino that night. Instead of putting on the red dress she had pulled out of the closet, she dressed simply in a grey pair of slacks, a white blouse, and a grey and pink sweater that she threw over her shoulders in case the night got chilly. She ran a comb quickly through her dark curls and put only the slightest bit of make-up beneath her eyes. Despite the healthy tan she had developed, she looked tired, a little fragile, thinner than she'd been. She stared at her face in the bathroom mirror and saw that the extra loss of weight had put slight hollows in her cheeks.

She thought it unattractive, not realising that it made her eyes appear larger, her mouth more vulnerable, the width of her brow more delicate beneath her cap of dark curls.

When she had finished dressing, she quickly left the boat and took to the streets of Rhodes, walking past the Hotel Athena where elegantly dressed guests poured in through the front doors, past the cafés with their chattering clientèle, past the numerous boutiques with their outdoor displays. She walked and walked, wanting to divert herself from her thoughts and lose herself in the shifting crowd. The first task was going to take some effort, but the second was easily accomplished. It didn't seem to matter to Rhodians that it was already nine at night; the street lamps were blazing so that it could have been daylight, and the streets were full of light-hearted partygoers and inquisitive tourists. The restaurants were full, and the boutiques were doing a rip-roaring business.

Samantha walked through the crowds, trying to fight off what she had learned about herself without any apparent success. It had been her decision about the casino that had suddenly exposed the shameful secret. She hadn't gone for two reasons. For one thing, she wasn't a gambler at heart. Secondly, she knew everyone else was going to be there, David included, and she had an extreme reluctance to see him again. Part of it was that she didn't know how she was going to fight off his advances with tact and gentleness any more. The other part was that she was truly afraid he would admit to having sent her the rose. While it would be nice to clear up the mystery, the knowledge that David was behind it would have disappointed Samantha immensely. To her horror, she had discovered that she much preferred to think Josh had made that romantic gesture.

And why is that? a little voice inside had asked her, and she couldn't ignore it no matter how hard she tried. The truth was that she was intrigued by Josh, she was fascinated by Josh and, yes, she wanted Josh. There it was. Admitted to. Out in the open. Despite everything he had put her through, despite every maddening statement and outrageous action, despite his obvious connection with the beautiful Helen, Samantha wanted him in a way she had never wanted anyone else. And nothing she could do altered the way she felt. She could talk to herself like a sympathetic but severe Dutch uncle, and it made no difference. She could become furious with herself, and it didn't matter one iota. For all her intelligence, her logic, and her control, she had, she realised, succumbed to one of nature's most basic impulses—raw physical desire.

It was humiliating, Samantha thought, as she wandered through the throng of tourists, a frown creasing her forehead, to discover that her mind had so little control over. . . well, to put it delicately— her matter. She had always believed that she was above such things, that she was too cool, too much in charge of her life. That had certainly been the case when she and Marshall had been lovers. Their relationship had been based less on physical desire than on a shared set of interests, classes and ambitions. They had studied together in law school, both being fascinated by contract law, and had even applied to many of the same legal firms after they had passed the bar. The attitude that had most characterised their affair had been one of detachment.

The irony was that Samantha had thought, at the time, that she was in love with Marshall and that he was in love with her. She had liked him from the first day of classes when he had sat behind her, a tall young man with reddish-brown hair and a sweet smile. Events had thrown them together, and the inevitable had occurred. Because their interests were so closely allied, they took more and more of the same classes. They were both asked to be on the staff of the college law review. Finally, in their third year of law school, they were put on to a huge project that involved hours of time together; weekends, evenings, meals. Then their housing arrangements fell apart. Samantha's room-mate had left school, leaving Samantha with the burden of too much rent; Marshall's room-mate planned to get married and wanted him to move out. It seemed only logical that they should join forces, share Samantha's rent and live together. Nobody in the outside world would have believed they weren't sleeping together before that, but the fact remained that their affair did not truly begin until after Marshall had moved into Samantha's apartment.

When she looked back on her relationship with Marshall, she could see how blind she had been to reality. Their sexual joining had more to do with convenience and propinquity than it had to do with love, desire or passion. Not having anything to measure it by, she had assumed that she and Marshall were in love. Oh, she'd been well aware that they weren't wildly infatuated with one another, but that hadn't seemed to matter at the time. They were so compatible mentally and temperamentally that she had never questioned the lukewarm tenor of their affair. In fact, both she and Marshall had even prided themselves on how different they were from their friends who had tempestuous and tumultuous love affairs. But all that cool emotion had only masked a truth that Samantha had not understood until years afterwards when she and Marshall had gone their separate ways—that there hadn't been love between them at all, just an intellectual friendship that hadn't even managed to survive the passing of time.

She stopped at a corner to wait while a car passed and thought how humbling it was to realise that she was no different from anyone else. She had always looked down her nose at women who let their emotions run their lives, who went into swoons over men, who spent hours agonising over their love affairs. She had thought she was above all that nonsense, but of course, she wasn't at all. The minute Josh had entered her life, the Samantha she had known had disappeared, and in her place was a woman of violent and infinitely changeable emotions. When she should have been reasonable, she had trembled with an unbelievable fury. When she should have resisted, she had succumbed with an overwhelming passion. And this new Samantha had been so naïve that it had taken her this long to figure out what would have been obvious to anyone else long ago—that all the emotion boiled down to one simple fact—she wanted to go to bed with Josh Sinclair.

At least, she was still pragmatic enough, she thought as she stepped across the street, not to elevate this blatant physical urge with something as noble and as edifying as love. She wasn't that senti-mental or romantic. What she felt was really very common and, while it couldn't exactly be ignored, it was possible that she could make some effort to act as if it didn't exist. She could, for example, start jogging around the boat's deck. She could take long sightseeing tours at every destination. She could torture herself with extremely cold showers. Whatever she did, it was clear that, one way or the other, she would have to suppress this unwanted physical longing. After all, Josh was already involved with another woman: in fact, they were probably sleeping together in Josh's new stateroom. Samantha allowed her vivid imagination to play that scene like a set of film takes. Josh with Helen in his arms. Josh and Helen in bed. Josh and Helen tangled together and . . . Samantha had thought she could toughen herself with these images, but they were so agonisingly painful that she quickly shut her eyes.

'Good God, are you trying to kill yourself?'

There was the screech of a car horn, a muttered Greek curse and the next thing Samantha knew was that she was standing back on the pavement with an angry Josh looking down on her, his hand gripping her arm with an iron fist.

'I . . .' she began.

'You walked right in front of that car. Didn't you look where you were going?'

'I guess I didn't.' But Samantha wasn't feeling at all abashed; what she was feeling was a euphoric sense of relief. He wasn't in bed with the beautiful Helen at all. He was standing next to her looking wonderfully attractive in a crisp pair of brown slacks, a white shirt and a beige jacket. One strand of dark hair fell across his forehead, and now he pushed it back impatiently, his fingers raking through the dark strands and tangling them in a delightful fashion.

He sighed and let go of her arm. 'Where are you going?' he asked.

'Nowhere in particular. I'm just wandering.'

'I thought you'd be at the casino.'

'I'm not much of a gambler,' she explained.

'No, neither am I.' He paused. 'Look, have you had any dinner?'

'No, I haven't, I. . .'

'Would you like to have dinner with me?'

Samantha was too taken aback to say anything. She'd been so sure that Josh would be spending all his waking hours with Helen that she had never once thought he would be out on his own. Not that his solitary appearance meant anything significant, she reminded herself. It was quite possible tht Helen was indisposed and had let him off for the evening. Or that they'd had a small lovers' tiff and. . .

'I know,' he added, 'that you can't stand my company.'

'Oh, no,' Samantha said hurriedly. 'It's quite all right.'

'You're sure?' he asked drily.

'Yes. Absolutely. Really, I don't mind at all.' It was very ironic that she, who could speak logically and incisively in business meetings and the courtroom, always took to babbling when Josh was around. It was as if his presence twisted or unravelled her brain connections. She made a supreme effort. 'Yes,' she said, 'dinner would be fine.'

They ate in a small restaurant called the Skorpios that featured a *bouzouki* player and an attentive, helpful waiter. To the background of music that sounded as if it had come directly from the soundtrack of *Zorba the Greek*, they managed to order a meal that included *tyropitta*, a cheese pie, as an appetiser, *kalamarakia*, baby squid, and *dolmades*, meat and rice wrapped in vine leaves, for the main course and *baklava* and Turkish coffee for dessert.

As if by mutual agreement, their conversation at the beginning of dinner was strictly non-personal. They discussed their new living arrangments. 'Enjoying your privacy?' Josh asked politely, and Samantha quickly nodded in agreement. 'Very much.' They talked casually about the cruise. 'Very relaxing,' Josh said, and Samantha added, Oh, yes, a wonderful vacation.' They compared notes on sightseeing, 'fabulous', on the ship's cook, 'fair', on the weather, 'glorious', and on the present restaurant which they both agreed was a find.

It wasn't until dessert that the conversation began to move in new and unsettling directions. Not that this was apparent at the outset; as their conversation turned to more personal matters, it took on, at first, a pleasurable air.

'You know, Samantha,' said Josh. 'I don't have a clue what you do for a living.'

'I don't know what you do either.'

'Shall we have a mutual confession?'

By this time, the *ouzo* she'd been sipping had gone slightly to Samantha's head. She shrugged. 'Why not?'

'Well, it could be quite devastating to discover that you're into plumbing and I dig ditches.'

'*Do* you dig ditches?'

He laughed. 'I'm in a related field—real estate.'

'Oh,' Samantha said, 'I should have known.'

He was smiling at her now—that lazy, sexy smile. 'Should you have?'

'That entrepreneurial air—that laid-back negotiating style.'

'I didn't know I possessed one.'

She tilted her head slightly as she gave him a critical look. 'Oh, yes,' she said, 'definitely.'

This was fun, she was thinking, this light-hearted, slightly flirtatious discussion with an attractive, desirable man. And he *was* attractive. In her anger at him, even in her desire for him, Samantha had quite forgotten just how attractive Josh was. The candle-light flickered across his face, emphasising the high line of a cheekbone, the strong line of his jaw, the depth of his eyes. For a second, she completely forgot that this was the Josh who was capable of driving her quite mad with anger, frustration and fury.

'And you?' he asked. 'Into plumbing?'

'Not even close,' she said. 'Guess again.'

He leaned back in his chair and studied her, one dark eyebrow slightly raised. 'Let's see,' he said. 'I'd have to go on what I know about you.'

'And what's that?'

'Mmm—that you're a bit on the serious side, very emotional and highly sensual.'

Samantha, who had been nibbling on her *baklava*, now choked. 'I beg your pardon?'

There was a humorous slant to his mouth. 'Serious, emotional and sensual.'

There was a lot of things that Samantha didn't like about this assessment of her character. True, she was serious, she'd always been that way, but she would never describe herself as 'very emotional'. That was patently absurd. She was cool, analytical, controlled—everyone knew that. And as for 'highly sensual'—well, she had better disabuse Josh of that dangerous notion immediately.

'Josh, that was a mistake,' she said quickly. 'We both agreed that it was a mistake.'

'What was?'

'That night. During the storm.'

'Oh, that.'

He was laughing at her again, she could tell by the amused glint in his eye. 'Now look,' she began hotly, 'I don't want you to think. . .'

'Sam.' Josh put one hand over the one she was waving furiously in the air. 'Why don't we just admit that we're attracted to one another!'

Samantha swallowed. 'Attacted to one another?' she echoed.

'Physically, sexually.'

She grabbed her hand out of his. 'No, I'm not,' she said stammering. 'You're not—we're not.'

Josh, damn him, was grinning. 'You're sure about that?'

The light, pleasurable flirtation was over, and Samantha had now remembered exactly who she was talking to. She ignored his question and said coldly, 'I'm a lawyer. I practise contract law.'

'Ah,' said Josh, 'then that accounts for it.'

'For what?'

'The façade of hard-headed pragmatism.'

'It's not a façade. I'm a very practical person.'

'Uh-uh.'

Samantha would have liked to know why Josh could make her more angry than anyone else. 'I am,' she said through clenched teeth.

'You know,' he said amiably, 'if that porthole hadn't blown open, you might be pregnant right now.'

She was shocked, but she wasn't good at court-room repartee for nothing. 'I'm on the pill,' she retorted.

'Nope, you're not.'

'How would you know?'

'I lived with you for five days. In fact, you don't have any contraceptive with you. Tell me, Sam, what *were* you going to do if you decided to go to bed with someone on the cruise?'

She was stunned, flabbergasted, tongue-tied. He had looked through her things; he'd examined her personal belongings! While she had assumed that he was ignoring her and acting as if she didn't exist, he'd been studying her intently, intimately, outrageously.

'Of course,' he went on as if what he'd said hadn't been shocking at all, 'you might have decided to leave it to the man, but that is a little dangerous, isn't it? It's the kind of thing one might do in the middle of an affair, but it would be risky with a stranger. Really, Sam, you have to take better care of yourself!'

Furious retorts sprang to her lips and died away. All she could manage after a moment of incoherent sounds was a hissed, 'How dare you search through my things?'

He leaned forward, his voice serious, a light gleaming in his eyes that had nothing to do with the candle flickering between them. 'I had a right to,' he said.

Her voice rose. 'A *right* to? You thought you had the right to dig through my belongings, to paw through my things, to. . .'

'Samantha,' he said softly, 'I want you.'

She should have continued to give him the well-honed, sharp side of her tongue. She should have slapped him hard across the face for being so impertinent. She should have stood up and stormed out of the restaurant. But she did none of these things, because, without warning, her body betrayed her. It softened, melted, flowed beneath the seductive force of his words. She felt a heat spread through her groin, and an aching begin at the very centre of her. And this sensation, this sudden surge of desire, was so

strong that it completely overwhelmed the part of her
that was telling her to get up, leave, get out.

She took a shaky breath. 'Josh, don't say that.'

'Why?'

'Because. . . it's not appropriate.'

'Why not?' His voice caressed her, moving over her
like a ripple of warm water.

She tried to explain even though she could barely
think straight. 'We hardly know one another. We
really don't get along. You. . . I. . . we're involved
with other. . .'

But he cut through her stammering, going right to
the heart of the matter, the core of her. 'Samantha,'
he said, stopping her stream of words, 'you want me,
too.'

Samantha couldn't help it; she visibly shuddered,
as if his words had, like an arrow, pierced her somewhere vital. She wanted to deny him, but she
couldn't. Desire had grown within her, invading her
veins, her bones, her muscles. Whatever anger she
had felt towards him had dissolved in this warmth,
this sudden, passionate warmth. An urgency to touch
him grew within her as if a physical contact, however
slight, could satisfy her craving for him. Samantha
forgot everything but that need, and she focused on
his mouth, those carved, slightly-parted lips that
seemed to beg for the caress of her fingers.

Helpless before such desire, she slowly lifted her
hand and moved it towards him. Time seemed to stop
as she reached for him, and she was aware of nothing
but his eyes, intent upon her, his mouth waiting for
her touch, his own hand now rising upward, the fingers long and lean, the hair dark on his muscular
wrist. Then suddenly reality intruded with the scrape
of a chair behind her, the raised voice of a diner, a

waiter passing by them, his speed causing their candle to waver. Her hand took flight then and jerked upwards as if it had come to the flame. She stood up, intending to leave, to run, to escape, but Josh's hand caught hers and she was held there, pinioned by his grasp.

'Let me go,' she said, her voice low and shaking.

His was huskier, harsh even. 'Not yet,' he said.

'Josh, please!'

He looked up at her. 'Think about what I said.'

'No, I. . .'

'Tomorrow,' he said firmly, 'we'll talk about it tomorrow.'

And then he did it. He turned her hand over so that it was palm upwards and raised it to his mouth, bending his head at the same time so that his mouth met the curve where her hand met her wrist, where the skin was tender and sensitive, where a pulse was beating as quickly as a hummingbird's heart. His lips touched her skin, and the touch reached deep within her, caressing her nerves, her muscles, the very bones of her hand. And then his tongue licked her in a hot, electrifying stroke, and she stiffened with shock as a flame of desire, more intense than she had ever known, shot down into her groin.

Samantha was, later, never able to figure out just how she managed to leave the Skorpios and get back to the *Princess Marguerita*. She remembered the agitation she felt as she dug through her purse and threw some drachmas on the table. She remembered the astonished look of the waiter as she darted past him and out on to the street. She would, she supposed, always have faint memories of street lamps going in a blur of illumination, of strange faces staring at her as she ran, of the hard feel of pavement beneath the delicate soles of her sandals. But she would never remember actually climbing the gangplank on to the ship and racing down to her room, or how she managed to find her key with such shaking hands and insert it in the lock. Memory only caught up with her when she was sitting on the couch in her darkened stateroom, trying her desperate best to sort it all out, to understand what had happened.

On a superficial level, it all seemed quite above board. Josh had asked her to dinner, he had flirted with her and then, in a logical sort of progression, he had made a pass at her. Samantha amended that— it was more than a pass, it had been a case of downright seduction. There had been sexy words, innuendoes, an invitation. His kiss on her hand— well, it would have looked quite innocent to an observer, a courtly, gallant, old-fashioned gesture. But it had really been something quite different. It had been a blatant statement of sensuality, a deliberate attempt to excite her.

The trouble was that—yes, she had been excited, so much so that she had had trouble breathing when it was all over. It had aroused memories in her mind that she had so carefully suppressed, memories of Josh's mouth on hers, his tongue at her breast, his hand between her legs. She had thought she had managed to obliterate those memories from her conscious mind, but now she discovered that, in fact, they had merely been lying below the surface, ready to rise into view the minute her guard was down.

Think about it, he had said. Well, she was thinking hard, and what she was thinking about made her more miserable than she had ever been in her life. For it had occurred to her that all Josh's moves, the rose (oh, yes, she was now sure it came from him), the sexy conversation, the seduction, the caress, were very strange. They reminded her of movies she'd seen, books that she'd read, but they did not remind her of anything that could happen in real life between two 1980s adults. They were stylised, artificial, calculated. They were exactly the sort of thing a man might do if he were being paid to be a romantic escort, if it were his job to provide her with seduction and excitement, if he had been hired by Fantasy Unlimited.

This was what Samantha was thinking, and every time she thought it, the logical part of her would deny it. This was the small, internal voice that laid out the evidence for her, provided the witnesses and made the logical conclusions. *You're crazy*, it said. *Mad. Nuts.* And that made more sense than her suspicions, because there was no way on God's green earth that Joshua Sinclair could be a paid escort from a company designed to provide clients with sexual fantasies made real. Other than his actions in the restaurant, he seemed a genuine article, a New Yorker who was in real estate, a. . . Samantha's mind paused in its whirl of confusion. . . well, what did she know about him anyway? Not a hell of a lot when she added the bits and pieces that she'd picked up all together. *That still doesn't make him a gigolo*, her internal voice said, and she had to concede that this was true. She was too acustomed to the due process of law to judge someone on circumstantial evidence.

And it occurred to her that the person she should be suspicious of was not Josh, but herself. She was the one who doubted, who could not believe that a man would treat her the way Josh had. Perhaps that doubt arose from her own insecurities, her own disbelief that a man would find her so attractive, so desirable and so sexy that he would send her flowers and act like a hero out of a romance novel. After all, Marshall had never acted that way, and she had assumed for many years that Marshall, affectionate but distant, was typical of most men. But what if he wasn't? What if there were men like Josh? What if dinner hadn't been a charade but the real thing? That thought made Samantha's head spin, because, despite her anger with him, her confusion and her shock, underneath she had loved every bit of it, had loved being with him, had loved. . .

Oh, no, she said to herself, don't get carried away on some idyllic romantic dream. That's what disillusion is made of—filmy hopes and unrealistic infatuations, self-deceit and wishful thinking. And she was no more in love with Josh than she was in love with the man in the moon. The attraction was strictly sexual, as he had said. He wanted her; she wanted him. That simple, basic equation of human lust. Which meant, of course, that she'd have to turn him down, because Samantha wasn't the type to get involved in an affair whose basis was less than love.

No, she thought, she would have to tell Josh no. He'd asked her to think it over, and she'd one so. Some of her thinking had been ridiculous—witness the spectre of Fantasy Unlimited raising its absurd head once again. But some of her thinking had been very careful, very logical. Samantha knew herself too well to take up Josh's offer. She was too vulnerable for a brief shipboard fling, a four-day romance that would end in Athens when they went their separate ways. She would hurt too much when it was so inevitably over. Even now, with only a seduction dangling before her, she had thought for a brief moment that she might be in love.

She stood up from the couch, clicked on the light and began to fold the sweater that she had been crushing in her abstracted hands. Her fingers had stopped quivering, her knees were no longer shaking, and her pulse rate had descended to something approaching normal. Thank heavens, she thought as she felt her usual calm come over her, for her powers of logic, her orderly rationality and her intellectual control. Thank heavens for those qualities that allowed her to reason things through, to come to the proper decisions and to pierce, with a cool internal eye, the gauzy, glittering curtain of dreams woven by her heart.

Her soft, foolish, ever-hopeful and very vulnerable heart.

CHAPTER NINE

JOSH stood naked before his bathroom mirror, a tall, lean figure with a broad chest, a narrow waist and muscles that had been bronzed to a high gleam by the sun. He was applying cologne to his freshly-shaved cheeks and humming to himself. His plans, he thought with the good humour of a man whose life is right on track, were all going well. Everything had clicked into place with the efficiency of a well-oiled machine. The groundwork had been set. The rules had been established. And the execution—well, that had been flawless, absolutely flawless. He had seen the results in Samantha's eyes, those wide blue eyes with the dark, thick lashes.

For a brief second, as he stared into the mirror, his face disappeared as Samantha's took its place. He saw the tumble of curls that framed her face, the softly parted mouth, the delicate but determined chin. A sweet face, a . . . he picked up his brush and ran it roughly through his hair. There was no point in getting sentimental about it, he chided himself. That would ruin his strategy, and he couldn't afford that. It would be too risky; he'd already learned what happened when you let your heart go one step further than it had ever gone before. It was like walking off a cliff. You could be strolling along, happy as a clam, thinking you were safe, satisfied with the world and your place in it and then—crash! You fell into the void without a net to catch you, arms to hold you, a voice to tell you that it was okay, that you weren't hurt, that the world hadn't come to a sudden end.

No, he couldn't have that happen again. He'd learned his lesson the hard way, and Josh was nothing if not a quick learner. He'd learned that a heart requires shielding to protect it from wounds and scars. He'd learned that the best armour was that of knowledge and cynicism and bitterness. And he'd also learned that attack was the best defence. His new philosophy, he thought as he wrapped a towel around his waist, was—go for what you want, but protect yourself from the consequences. And that was precisely what he was doing.

On the other hand, he hadn't quite thought it would be so much fun. *Honest-to-goodness romantic sincerity,* Marybeth had advised David about Samantha. Well, Josh had never given much thought to being romantic before, he'd never considered himself as a swashbuckling figure capable of making a woman forget her denials and inhibitions. But he'd taken to the role the way a duck takes to water—in fact, he was beginning to think he was a natural at it. Flowers, invitations, sexy words, smouldering looks—he'd known just how to make Samantha feel that she was desired above everything else. And the scheme was working beyond all his wildest expectations. *She can't stand the sight of him*, Marybeth had also said to David, *you don't have to worry about him.* Josh gave a short, harsh laugh as he stepped out into his bedroom. He'd be able to blow that theory sky-high by the time he was done. When he was finished with Samantha, she'd be so bedazzled and infatuated that David what's-his-name might as well not have existed at all.

It never occurred to a smug and satisfied Josh that there might be other, less obvious, motives behind his pursuit of Samantha. The thought that he might be involving himself in a relationship that went beyond the purely sexual never entered his mind.

No—as he began to dress, Josh had no suspicion that all was not as it had been and that he was no longer the same man who had boarded the *Princess Marguerita* . Warning bells didn't ring in his head. His subconscious was quiet and docile and passive. All he felt was a self-deceiving belief that he knew precisely what he was doing, a pleasure in his forth-coming success, and an intoxicating sense of anticipation. Once again there was a memory of Samantha, not of her face this time, but of her body over his in that dark stateroom, the feel of her soft breasts against his chest, the silky skin of her legs beneath his hand. And the memory brought a smile to his lips and a gleam to his eyes—the predatory gleam of a hunter who has his victim squarely in his sights and is now heading in for the kill.

A conversation was taking place between Marybeth and David on the bustling pier where the *Princess Marguerita* was docked. They had descended the gangplank and were walking together, their heads as close together as two heads can be when the people in question stand six foot two and five foot two respectively in their stockinged feet.

'Was Samantha at breakfast?' he was asking.

Marybeth shook her head and frowned. 'No.'

'Do you think she's with someone else? I mean, she wasn't at the casino last night either.'

'Well, I don't know who it would be,' Marybeth said. 'I really don't.'

David gave an unhappy sigh. 'She seems to have disappeared into thin air.'

'And after you sent her that rose, too. It doesn't seem right.'

He stopped and looked down at her. 'What rose?'

'Why, the rose that . . . David! Didn't you send Samantha that lovely rose?'

'No, I. . .'

'Hadn't we agreed on flowers?'

'Yes, but I thought I'd give them to her when I saw her. There's always people selling flowers on the street.'

'Well then, who on earth . . .?'

'I know who it is,' David said morosely. 'That guy—the one who shares her stateroom.'

Marybeth's blue eyes had a musing, faraway expression. 'I wonder,' she began, then said, '. . . I doubt it. I really do.'

'But . . .'

Marybeth made an impatient sound. 'And even if he did—well, it doesn't necessarily mean a thing. They're not sharing a stateroom any more and it could have just been a gesture.' She paused. 'On the other hand, there is a possibility that . . .'

'See,' said David, 'even you admit that there's a good chance she'd fall for him.'

But she would have none of it. She gave a quick, firm shake of her blonde curls and said, 'David, this is where we separate the men from the boys and the chaff from the wheat.'

'The chaff from the . . . what are you talking about?'

'Plan B,' Marybeth said ominously.

David gave her an amused look. 'Plan B?'

'Uh-uh.'

'It sounds dangerous.'

'It is,' she said.

'And risky.'

She nodded solemnly. 'The whole thing could blow up in our faces—sky-high. Honeybunch, are you a gambling man?'

'Am I a gambling man?' he appealed to the sky. 'I lost two hundred drachmas last night and she asks me if I'm a gambling man!'

She gave him a tiny slap on the shoulder. 'This is a serious matter,' she said. 'No fooling around.'

He assumed an expression of matching solemnity. 'Lead on,' he said.

Marybeth looked carefully around them, checking out the faces of passers-by, the street ahead and if anyone they knew was behind them. When she was confident that no one could overhear them, she began, 'Tonight at the dance . . .'

'Are you sure she'll be there?'

'The ship's sailing at midnight. Of course she'll be there. Now, listen.'

'I'm all ears.'

'Tonight, at the dance . . .'

The subject of this conversation had no idea that plans were being concocted on her behalf. Instead, she was standing on the ancient acropolis of Lindos and staring down a sheer cliff of white rock to the turquoise of the Aegean Sea. A slight froth swirled at this meeting of solid and liquid, but she was too high to hear the sound of the waves. What Samanatha couldn't hear, however, she could see. The ancient town had been built on a high promontory that jutted out into the water, and the clarity of the air allowed her to see for miles. Behind her were the

scrubby hills. Below her was the modern town of
Lindos whose white houses clustered like child's
blocks around the sandy harbour. And in front of her
was the huge arc of the sea; a brilliant turquoise that
shaded erratically into aquamarine or a deep rich
green, its horizon merging with the sky whose own
intense hue was lightened by the gleaming yellow of
the sun.

Samantha sighed at the beauty of it, considered her
day trip out of Rhodes to have been worth the effort
and the cost of the taxi ride, and didn't hear the foot-
steps behind her. She sat down on the wall that
overlooked the sea, oblivious to the shadow that was
cast across her feet. And so engrossed was she in her
contemplation of the scenery that she almost didn't
hear the voice that said, 'When you see it like this you
can understand why the ancient Greeks would build
their town here. It's completely defensible; they could
pick off the enemy sailors like flies.'

Samantha turned slowly, very slowly, to face the
man behind her. He wore a white T-shirt that fitted
snugly to his broad chest, faded jeans with form-fit-
ting hip pockets, and aviator sunglasses that
emphasised a strong nose and the hard line of his jaw.
He was hatless, and his hair was dark and gleaming
in the sun. Irrationally, the very first thought that
came into her mind was how handsome he was and,
with it that yearning, melting and totally unwanted
sensation of desire.

He gestured towards the low brown hills. 'And
enemy soldiers as well. Think of it like a Cecil B. De
Mille film with a cast of thousands pouring out of the
hills.'

Fortunately for Samantha, second thoughts had
quickly followed her first ones, and those were tinged,

not with desire, but with a mounting irritation and
an uneasy sense of fear. She felt as if she were being
pursued, as if Josh were tracking her down, as if he
were the hunter and she were the victim. The combination of emotions made her clench her teeth and
say accusingly, 'What are you doing here?'

Josh grinned his lazy smile at her. 'Sightseeing,
what else?'

Third thoughts had whirled through her brain,
suspicious and wary thoughts, visions of conspira-
cies and cabals. 'You followed me.' she said flatly.

'Tch-tch.' He took off his glasses and sat down
beside her. 'Now, isn't that a bit paranoid, Sam?' He
shook his head gravely. 'Not a good character trait
for a lawyer, I would think.'

A cold fury enveloped her. It wiped out any lin-
gering remnants of her first, second and third
thoughts. 'I am *not* paranoid,' she said icily, 'I just
find it very peculiar that you and I should end up precisely in the same spot when . . .' She paused, not
quite willing to admit that she had gone to certain
lengths to avoid him.

'When . . .?' he asked encouragingly.

'Let's just say that I think it's odd.'

'Life is odd,' Josh said calmly. 'Haven't you ever
noticed? It's full of coincidences, peculiar moments
and strange happenings.'

'I really don't think there's anything coincidental
in the fact that you and I are . . .'

'And that's the beauty of it,' he went on as if she
hadn't uttered a word. 'Think how boring life would
be if it weren't for these moments.'

Samantha immediately recognised what she had
come to think of as a 'Josh-ism'; a conversational
gambit, a switching of gears in the middle of a dis-

cussion, a turn down a digressionary path that would lead her away from the very goal towards which she was heading. Well, she wasn't going to let him get away with it this time!

'You think you're very clever, don't you?'

'Well,' he said modestly, 'in my field, some people have seemed to think that my. . .'

'I am *not* talking about your field,' Samantha said furiously. 'I'm talking about the way you always change the direction of the conversation.'

'In what way?' he asked innocently.

'Whenever. . . oh, the hell with it.' She stood up, threw the strap of her bag over her shoulder and spoke a blatant lie. 'I hope you have a nice day.'

Josh was up in a moment, his hands taking hers, his body an obstacle in her path. 'Samantha,' he said with concern, 'what's the matter?'

'Nothing.'

'You're all upset.'

'I. Am. Not. Upset!'

But it was another lie. She was upset; she could feel her face flushing and her breathing coming in a rapid, uneven tempo. For a person of non-violence, she was demonstrating all sorts of alarming symptoms. Her hands, caught in his, itched to be free so that she could throttle him. The toes of one foot yearned to kick him in the shins, the heel of the other would have liked to grind his foot into the hard ground. The fact was, she wanted to kill him.

Samantha had never had the urge to murder any-one in her life, and that upset her even more. She grabbed her hands out of his, turned on her heel and tried to march swiftly away, not caring whether or not he followed her. But the acropolis of Lindos was against her. The ground was littered with the debris of centuries, and she had to step awkwardly over stones, rock, pieces of broken walls, jagged bits of fallen columns. In order to keep her balance she had to walk with her arms outstretched, and one of these was taken firmly by Josh.

'Easy does it . . . watch your step here, that stone is wobbly. Here, hold on tight . . . it'll make the going down easier.'

Which was how Samantha found herself walking hand-in-hand with Josh past the broken temple of Artemis, through the ceiling-less rooms of the medieval castle and down the steep steps towards town where old women in black sat on lawn chairs, displaying hand-made lace doilies, napkins and tablecloths spread out to entice the eye of the tourist. It was a very silent journey. Even Josh had stopped speaking. They were, Samantha thought with a feeling of surrender, communicating through their clasped hands. At first, his had been firm, holding hers tightly, not allowing her to pull away. Her hand had been tense, holding itself still, trying to ignore the warm circle of his fingers. Then, she had relaxed in spite of herself and he, sensing her yielding, had laced his fingers through hers in a companionable sort of way. It was all very strange, oddly comfortable and surprisingly non-threatening. By the time they had reached the town centre, Samantha had discovered that she was no longer angry with Josh.

'Here we are,' he said.

She looked around her. 'Where?'

'At my car.'

She looked at the small red Fiat. 'You rented a car?'

'And,' he said with a flourish as he opened the back door, 'I've got a picnic lunch, a beach blanket and an umbrella.'

Now that she was no longer angry with him, her sense of humour had reasserted itself. 'And all you need is the girl to go along with it?'

He grinned at her. 'You guessed.'

'The truth now,' said Samantha. 'Are you going to tell me the truth about our meeting here?'

'Nope, I want to leave you in suspense.'

'Josh . . .' she began.

'No questions,' he said firmly as he ushered her into her car. 'Just let yourself go with the flow.'

Going with the flow meant obediently sitting on her side while he got in his and started the ignition. It meant letting him drive away from Lindos without asking where they were going. And it meant taking surreptitious looks at his profile and wondering what was going on behind that handsome façade.

During one of those looks, he glanced at her, and she quickly looked back out at the passing scenery. 'You know something, Sam,' he said in a teasing voice, 'I don't think I've ever seen you so quiet. Are you sure you're okay?'

'Count your blessings,' she said tartly, 'it won't last.'

'Ah,' he said with a laugh, 'there's the Samantha that I know—tough as nails!'

'I'm not usually like that,' she retorted.

'No?'

'No, you bring out the worst in me.'

'The worst?'

'I don't know why that is,' she went on. 'Although it just might be your personality.'

Josh shrugged as he pulled the car around a man in a cart which was being pulled by a donkey. 'I don't think so,' he said. 'I have quite a pleasant personality.'

'What a surprisingly unprejudiced remark!'

Her sarcasm didn't faze him in the least. In fact, it seemed to have the opposite effect of invigorating him, and Samantha realised that he was enjoying this repartee immensely.

'Oh, I'm an extremely unprejudiced person,' he told her. 'My heart is open to members of all races, colours and creeds. I'm the kind of guy who takes in starving kittens and orphaned puppies.'

The trouble was, she was enjoying it, too. 'Why don't I believe you?'

'Because you don't know me,' he said. 'You've been blind to my sterling qualities.'

'Which are?'

'Integrity, good humour, reliability, patience, forthrightness, generosity to a fault,' he was warming to his subject now, 'a pillar of the community, a good citizen, a man whose actions prove him to be . . .'

'Dishonest and cunning.'

'Ouch,' he said. 'You have a very low opinion of me.'

'The evidence points in that direction.'

'A man is innocent until he's proved guilty.'

'Did you or did you not follow me to Lindos?' Samantha demanded.

'I didn't follow you.'

'Yes, you did,' she said hotly. 'You . . .'

'I came before you.'

Indignation seeped out of her like air out of a deflated balloon. 'Oh!'

He gave a shrug. 'I just bribed your steward so I could find out where you were going. He told me that you were planning on a day sightseeing in Lindos and sunbathing at a beach.'

'There,' she said triumphantly. 'I knew it!'

He gave her an amused, sideways glance. 'And you're flattered.'

'Of course not,' she said with asperity. 'I consider this a form of abduction.'

'And you hate every minute of it.'

'Every single minute.'

'I'll have to see what I can do about that, won't I?'

Samantha refused to be beguiled by the innuendo in that statement. 'I doubt if you'll be able to change my mind, Mr Sinclair.'

'We'll see, Miss 93rd Street,' he said with a smile. 'We'll see.'

They parked by a small, deserted cove whose beach was hidden by a ridge of low hills. It was an idyllic spot with an expanse of white sand, water lapping gently at the shoreline, and a solitary gull or two swooping overhead. Occasionally ships passed along the horizon, their stacks or sails visible only at a distance, but there was no sign of human visitation other than a Coke bottle that washed up and down against the shore.

Within a short time, however, they had established a small oasis of humanity on that isolated beach. The umbrella had been raised, its green and red stripes making a gay splash of colour against the brown of the hills. The beach blanket, a wool plaid whose colours had faded with time, was spread out beneath it so that one corner was in the shade. There Josh placed the cooler that held a picnic lunch. And there he neatly folded his jeans, his T-shirt, his belt, his socks and his sandals. Beneath his clothes, he'd worn a brief blue bathing suit.

Samantha ignored the enticing way his muscles rippled in the sun as he moved and said primly,

'Please turn around while I get changed.'

'You know,' he said as he obediently turned, 'we could have gone to one of the nude beaches.'

'What?' she asked as she pulled her dress over her head.

'Nude beaches.'

'Nude as in naked?'

'Uh-uh.'

Samantha tied the halter top of her bikini on. 'As in completely and utterly naked?' she asked, and tried to imagine herself sunbathing in the nude. It was bad enough to think of wearing nothing in a crowd, but it was worse when she contemplated sharing a beach blanket with a man who wasn't a husband or a lover. How, she wondered, does one hold up one's end of the conversation when the other participant is lounging around in what is euphemistically referred to as his 'birthday suit'? Where in heaven's name does one look? Up, she supposed with a touch of amusement, up, not down. Never down.

'Completely,' Josh said. 'That's what they tell me.'

'Who's they?'

'Well, actually, the steward.'

'He doesn't tell *me* things like that.'

' 'You mean he didn't tell you about the massage parlour or the topless night club or the place that sells dirty movies?'

Samantha slipped out of her briefs and pulled on her bikini bottom. 'I had no idea Rhodes was such a den of iniquity,' she said coldly, and then added, 'You can turn around now—I'm done.'

But as he turned, she quickly knelt down on the blanket and began to fold her dress. She didn't want to see Josh's expression or have him comment in any way on what she looked like in a bikini. The truth was that, beneath the idle banter and casual flirtation, there were different messages being passed, and Samantha wasn't quite sure what she was agreeing to or what would happen. They hadn't discussed their mutual attraction, the conversation had only skirted around the issue of sex. But here they were together, in the briefest of clothes, on what amounted to a desert island, with nothing to stop them from consummating that attraction. Samantha wouldn't have admitted it to a soul, but she was nervous, more nervous than she'd ever been in her life

If Josh sensed her state of nerves, he gave no indication of it for the next hour. All through their picnic lunch, he treated her as if she were a sexless companion, a pal on an outing, a friendly acquaintance. As they sipped white wine and nibbled at crackers topped with lobster pâté, they discussed nothing more important than the weather, a book they had read, a movie both of them had seen. The sun was strong enough by early afternoon to have them both in the sea where Josh set out on a long swim and Samantha stood waist-high, splashing water on her neck and shoulders, as she watched him cut through the waves, his arms moving rhythmically, his kick even and powerful.

'You're good,' she said when he swam back and stood up near her, his hair sleeked back, droplets of water coursing over his shoulders and chest. 'You must do a lot of swimming.'

'I'm in a club,' he told her.

'A swimming club?' she asked as they walked back to the blanket and lay down on it.

Josh rolled on to his back and closed his eyes against the sun. 'Yup—a competitive club.'

'Do you go in for races?'

'Occasionally.'

Samantha lay down on her stomach, resting her head on her arms, her face turned in his direction. What she could see of him was a brown, curved shoulder, the curl of his ear, tangled dark hair and the crescent of one eyelash that lay across his cheek. She contemplated him for a moment and then curiosity overcame her. 'What else do you do?' she asked.

'What do you mean—what else?'

'You swim and work and—what else?'

'I suppose you're talking about women.'

She was flustered. 'Well, I   ...'

'When a women wants to know what a man does,' he said calmly, his eyes still closed, 'she's really asking about his sex life.'

'You think you know everything, don't you?'

'A lot,' he said. 'Not everything.'

'Well, for your information,' Samantha lied, 'I couldn't care less.'

'You're sure about that?'

'Yes.'

'Then you'd rather not know about Helen?'

'Helen?' she queried.

Of the red hair and manic sex drive.'

It was impossible for Samantha to maintain her nonchalance. Her head came up off her arms. 'What do you mean?'

He grinned up towards the sun. 'I thought you couldn't care less.'

'Well, that's an incredible thing to say about someone!'

'Is it?' he asked lazily. 'She was always trying to lure me into bed.'

Samantha carefully put her head back, only this time she stared in the opposite direction, facing the stretch of beach. 'And were you lured?' she asked in an equally lazy voice.

'Do I detect a smidgin of interest, Miss 93rd Street?'

She could tell from his voice that he had turned on to his side and was now looking at her, but nothing on earth could have made her face him. 'Other people's sex lives are always interesting in a clinical sort of way,' she said.

'True,' he replied. 'For example, you once told me that men are insensitive. I wondered where you did your research.'

'You didn't answer my question,' Samantha returned. 'I'm not going to answer yours.'

'All right,' said Josh. 'A question for a question, an answer for an answer. Fair enough?'

She tried to analyse it. The law had taught her that questions could be asked in different ways to elicit different answers. They could be probing, angled, direct or oblique. A skilful questioner could always learn more than the person questioned wished to reveal. And then, of course there were answers that could be phrased to camouflage reality, to avoid telling the truth, to turn the questioner in the wrong direction. If Josh were clever, she'd learn nothing. If she were clever, he'd learn nothing. On the other hand, suppose she gave something away and he didn't? Wouldn't that put her at an uncomfortable disadvantage? She tried to frame a statement about the need to be honest during the coming exchange, but the sun was too hot and the heat made her head swim a bit.

It just seemed easier to answer him, so she turned to face him and discovered that her head had gone from swimming to drowning. He was too close to her and, with his body angled sideways, she was given the long view; of a muscular throat, a deep chest, black hair angling across a flat abdomen, unexplored and enticing terrain beneath the narrow triangle of blue silk. She had to make a deliberate effort to raise her eyes to the level of his, to confront the lazy grin that told her without words that he knew precisely what she was doing, to actually remember what she'd been about to say.

She cleared her throat. 'All right, a question for a question, an answer for an answer.'

'I wasn't lured into her bed,' he said.

The sun, the heat and the overdose of masculinity almost had Samantha bemused enough not to catch the hole in that answer, but her laywer's training saved her. The hole was so big you could have driven a truck right through it. After all, what she really wanted to know was if Josh had made love to Helen, and the act could have taken place anywhere—his bed, her bed. 'You mean, you didn't sleep with her?' she asked.

'It's my turn,' he said. 'You'll have to wait. Tell me, have you ever had an affair?'

She discovered that *she* didn't want to be honest. Oh, she wanted to know everything about Josh there was to learn, but she didn't want him privy to her own secrets. But his question was direct and unavoidable and, reluctantly, she said, 'Yes.'

'Your turn.'

'Did you sleep . . .' Samantha caught the imprecision and corrected herself, 'have sex with Helen?'

'No. Did you love him?'

Samantha felt such a rush of relief at the knowledge that Helen's insinuations had been lies that she'd lost track of the conversation. 'Who?' she asked.

'The man you had an affair with.'

'No, I . . . I didn't love him.' There was an odd flicker in Josh's eyes. 'Have you ever been married?'

'No. Then why did you have an affair with him?'

It was going too fast for her. She could barely digest the answer before she was confronted with another question. 'I thought I loved him.'

'Did he love you?'

The sun, the intensity of his eyes, the heat was making her so dizzy that she forgot that it was her turn to ask, her turn to probe and dig. 'No,' she said, 'he didn't.' And she put her head face down into the circle of her arms. It felt good to close her eyes and not have the brilliance of the sun making her eyelids feel as thin as paper. It felt even better to end a conversation that had brought back unpleasant and unhappy memories. And, above all, it felt wonderful to obliterate the vision of Josh for a few minutes and allow her head to clear.

As she lay there, Samantha realised that she had made a very bad and very dangerous decision when she had agreed to spend the day with Josh. She'd known that she was attracted to him, but in her naïveté she had believed she could keep the attraction under control. And she was so accustomed to her lawyer-like clarity of mind that it had never occurred to her that the closeness of any man could make her so dizzy that she would forget what she was saying or what she was doing. She wanted to blame it on the sun and the heat, but the symptoms hadn't begun until she'd turned her head and found him only inches away, his bare flesh so close to hers that it had taken every bit of will power she had to keep from drawing nearer.

The best thing she could do, she decided in the dark circle of her arms, was to bring this outing to an end.

If it went on much longer, if he got any closer to her, she was no longer sure that she'd be in control. And if there was one thing that terrified her above anything else, it was being out of control. Therefore the thing to do was to get up and demand that Josh take her back to the *Princess Marguerita*. If he refused, she would say she had a vicious headache, a sore throat, a fever, whatever it would take to convince him that she couldn't spend one more moment on the beach without collapsing.

This last thought was so pleasing to her that she decided to bypass the first step and move right into a devastating illness. Faintness, she decided, that would do it. She'd sit up and announce that she was feeling faint. And the truth was that she was feeling the slightest bit faint anyway, wasn't she? Besides, it was quite possible that the moment she opened her eyes again, the dizziness would return. She imagined that moment. She'd find Josh in front of her, his eyes dark and intent, his flesh so close she could feel his heat on her own, his . . . God, she was feeling dizzy and faint already! She wouldn't even be faking it.

Samantha was so pleased with herself that she smiled into the darkness and almost didn't feel his palm sliding across her skin and the slight tug on the strap of her halter. It was seconds before it came home to her that he had actually undone the bow at the back, thereby making her top absolutely useless. She started to protest, but now his hands were moving lower to the brief wisp of fabric that stretched across her hips. It was held in place to the front piece of fabric by two bows. Actually, Samantha thought dizzily, they were knots. She hadn't wanted to make bows every time she put the bikini on, so she'd made knots. Good, strong knots. Knots that would have made her Girl Scout leader proud. Knots that could have held a ship to a dock in a high wind. Knots that should have made her feel secure and safe and protected—instead of naked and vulnerable, faint and helpless, afraid and yet so wanting that she did not move, did not even breathe as his hands moved ever lower.

CHAPTER TEN

'YOU'RE burning up,' Josh said.

'I am?' Samantha's voice was a strangled whisper.

His fingers inched down the edge of her bikini. 'You're turning red.'

'Oh.'

Then she felt a cool application of suntan lotion on her back and the soothing strokes of his hands as he spread it along the upper muscles of her arms and then, in broad caresses, on the curve of each shoulder. His hands drew together as they reached the indentation of her spine, and he worked the lotion with his fingers down each side of her backbone.

When he began on her legs, Samantha tried to ignore what was happening to her. She lay absolutely still, acting as if his fingers were not on her calves or the back of her knees, behaving as if she didn't care when his hands moved to her thighs, their circling motion bringing him ever closer to that soft juncture of skin between her legs. When his fingers brushed the fabric of her bikini, she steeled herself against moving, but when it happened again, she could not stop the sound that escaped her lips.

'Turn over,' he said huskily, and Samantha couldn't stop herself. Obediently, she turned over, one forearm flung over her eyes to blot out the sun, the other braced across her chest to conceal what her untied halter could no longer cover.

He began with her toes and the arches of her feet,

caressing the delicate bones of her ankles, holding each foot between his hands and bestowing on them his undivided attention. The gentle caressing of his fingers was a precursor of what was to come, and Samantha held herself breathless against the moment when his hands would move up her legs. And then, when it happened, the sensation was so erotic that her legs actually parted slightly to make his voyage easier. But she shivered when he touched the insides of her thighs and, sensing her tension, he moved upward, his thumbs running along the edge of her hipbones and then sweeping across the soft swell of her abdomen.

A warm dizziness came over her when he gently removed her arm from its protective stance across her chest and tossed the now useless halter aside. She felt her nipples harden as his hands spread across her rib cage and then moved upwards to cup her breasts which seemed to swell in anticipation of her caress.

'Josh,' she said. 'Oh, Josh.' And then he took her in his arms, his bare skin touching hers, his lips meeting hers, their bodies touching at toe, knee, hip, chest. Nothing remained of Samantha except the passion that had now taken over her.

Josh lifted his mouth from hers. 'God,' he swore, 'not again!'

Without the protection of his head to keep the sun off her face, Samantha was forced to turn her head to one side. It was then that she caught what he had heard; the revving of a car motor just before it clicked off, the blaring music of a radio, high-pitched laughter, doors slamming, a child crying—all the sounds of the arrival of a group of people who have come to enjoy the beach on a hot afternoon.

'Oh, lord!' she breathed, sitting up quickly,

grabbing for her halter and holding it up against her, her fingers shaking as she tried to do up the ties.

'Easy,' Josh said softly. 'I'll fix it.' His fingers were far steadier than hers and, when he touched her, he could feel that she was trembling. 'Will you be all right?' he added.

She nodded, although she had no idea when that would be true. She was still shaking; her very skin felt as if it were quivering. Desire, she found, does not disappear at will. It can come unannounced, creeping up on you, a saboteur out to destroy your calm, well-ordered life. It wasn't until the family of noisy beachgoers had appeared with their paraphernalia, and she and Josh had cleaned up the remains of their stay, that Samantha actually began to erect around herself some of the walls and defences that made up her usual air of composure.

She walked to the car, her legs steady.

She helped Josh pack the picnic basket, umbrella and blanket in the trunk.

She discussed the sudden increase of traffic on the road back to Rhodes.

She sat beside him and acted as if nothing untoward had happened on that lovely, isolated beach.

In fact, she was just beginning to breathe a little easier and to feel as if she were once again back in control of her life, when the realisation hit her, like a blow, an attack, an explosion. It destroyed the very shaky barricade of calm she had erected. It blew apart the theories about herself that she had always taken as gospel. It made her sit up, rigid, in the car seat and stare fixedly and unseeingly at the suburbs of Rhodes. What had finally hit her was so obvious, it was a wonder that she had not realised it before, but then she had spent so much time lying to herself, trying to cover up what was happening, and attempting to shield herself from vulnerability, that she'd managed to avoid the truth.

She had fallen in love.

The dizziness came over her again, forcing her to grab on to the handle of the car door, but it didn't blur the clarity of the evidence. Everything pointed to the verdict—the emotional swings she'd had ever since meeting Josh, the way she lost control every time she ended up in his arms, her overwhelming desire to sleep with him. No man had ever made her feel that way. In fact, in her heart of hearts, Samantha had even wondered if she'd been born so careful and cautious that she was incapable of falling in love. But Josh had proved to her otherwise and, while there was a part of her that gloried in the knowledge that she could be like everyone else, that she had finally fallen truly in love, and that the object of her desire was sitting only inches away from her, the other part was well aware that there was absolutely no cause for celebration.

'Well,' said Josh when he had managed to manoeuvre the car into a comfortable spot between a truck and a taxi, 'we're going to have to do something about this.'

She didn't dare look at him—not with her new knowledge. 'I don't think you can,' she said. 'It must be rush hour.'

He gave her an amused look. 'I'm not talking about the traffic.'

'Oh,' she said, and glanced down at her inter-twined hands.

'I'm talking about us.'

'Let's not talk about it.'

'Why not?'

'Because . . . because I'm sorry it ever happened.'
He was infuriatingly calm. 'No, you're not.'

'I am!'

'You enjoyed it as much as I did.'

Samantha couldn't deny that, but she could
certainly refuse the next opportunity for enjoyment.
'I don't want to ever . . .' she began hotly.

'Look, Sam, I'm not going to push you into
anything you don't want. That's not my style, so
you don't have to worry about it. And I'd like to
think that, if and when we do make love together,
you're there of your own free will.' The traffic was
too heavy for him to give her anything more than a
quick look. 'I'm not going to pressure you. It's up
to you to come to me. All right?'

His words were so thoughtful, so gentle and so
caring that for a brief second Samantha allowed
herself to be deceived into believing that what Josh
proposed was not a shipboard fling, but a longer,
more enduring relationship. After all, she thought
as another wave of dizziness passed over her, they
didn't live far from one another in New York; in
fact, they were practically neighbours. There was no
reason why the emotions engendered between them
under the hot Greek sun couldn't be continued and
nurtured in the hustle and bustle of their normal,
daily lives. She saw herself going out with Josh to
the theatre, spending Sunday mornings with him
reading *The New York Times*, holding hands as they
strolled down Riverside Park. She saw them sharing
an apartment together, meeting one another's
families, making decisions about marriage and
children and careers. The vision was so glorious that
it even went one absurd step further, and she saw
herself holding a baby in her arms, a baby with dark
hair and Josh's dark eyes and . . .

No! Josh wasn't offering her love or marriage; he was extending the invitation to spend a few nights with him, to let her hair down and go a bit wild, to take on the role of the lover in a brief and very artificial play. He didn't want commitment; he wanted a few days of fun and games, a diversion, a satisfactory conclusion to his vacation. Samantha felt her sweet fantasy shatter and crack like a picture that is dropped from a great height, its shards of glass, splintered and cutting, exploding in every direction.

'All right?' Josh asked again.

Samantha came back to the reality of the small, hot car, the dry wind blowing in her face from the opened window, the sounds of roaring traffic in her ears. Well, she thought wryly, she wouldn't commit herself to anything either. Love might have dimmed her instinct for caution, but it hadn't entirely distinguished her instincts of self-preservation. All she had to do, she decided, was keep herself away from such dangerous places as the bedrooms of staterooms and isolated beaches.

'Yes,' she said, 'all right.' And because her voice was so flat and calm, Josh glanced at her again. Samantha could feel his curious scrutiny, but she kept her eyes on the road, her back straight and her head held high, not knowing that the delicate sweetness of her profile made something catch in his throat and caused him to look quickly away as if she had suddenly become too bright for his eyes, far too brilliant to bear.

It was the theory of safety in numbers that made Samantha decide to go to the dance that night, despite that fact she was still having bouts of dizziness as well as the occasional cold spell followed by

the sensation that she was hot and flushed. It would
have been wiser, she supposed, to crawl into bed
and suffer, but she couldn't bear the idea of spending
hours in her own company, arguing with herself
about Josh, contemplating her own misery. Besides,
she was rarely ill and, when the occasional 'flu
struck, she'd always managed to shrug it off with
the ease of someone who is blessed with good health.
So she took two aspirins and put on her pale yellow
dress, the one with filmy long sleeves and a tailored,
collared neckline that contrasted strongly with its
flowing skirt. A bit of cover-up hid the mauve circles
beneath her eyes, and she could thank the tan she'd
got for the rest. The woman in the bathroom mirror
who stared back at her looked as if she had stepped
out of a bandbox.

The *Princess Marguerita* was due to leave that
night for Crete. Its gangplank had been drawn up,
and its crew were making preparations for depar-
ture. The ballroom was crowded. When Samantha
entered, she was immediately assaulted by a kalei-
doscope of colours and sounds, the lanterns strung
across the ceiling vying in hue and shade with the
women's dresses, the hum of vivacious chatter filling
the air between the beat of drums and the pause of
the band.

It took Samantha a while to distinguish strangers
from acquaintances, partly because of the crowd and
partly because when she did so, the first identifica-
tion came as something of a shock. She had to blink
to make sure she wasn't seeing things, and then
stepped forward in order to assure herself that she
wasn't making a mistake. Not five feet in front of
her was a table tucked away in a corner and, at that
table, were two people. Their being together was not
the surprise in itself, since David and Marybeth had

been thrown together in one another's company so many times that there was no reason why they shouldn't share a table. No, it was what they were doing that rooted Samantha to the spot where she was standing.

They were engaged in a kiss.

And the kiss was not your garden variety that grew out of affectionate friendship. It was a full-blown, passionate kiss, with hands tangled in hair, bodies pressed together, mouths clinging to one another like limpets. The odd thing about it was that Samantha could have sworn that Marybeth had seen her before the kiss had started. Not that she minded, of course. In fact, she felt a surge of relief that David had finally found someone who was receptive to his advances. It just had never crossed her mind that that someone would be Marybeth, but then weren't shipboard romances supposed to be like that?

The proof of that hypothesis was to be found as she headed by the corner of the dance floor and found Betty swirling past her. She gave Samantha a small smile over her partner's shoulder and a little wave before she was danced back into the crowd. Samantha had to stop once more, blink and then wonder how so much had taken place under her nose without her being aware of it all. Certainly, the very last person she would have expected Betty to be dancing with was—the purser of Vulcan Cruise Lines. The hand-wringing, spectacled and mousta-chioed purser.

What else? Samantha thought as a dull throbbing began in her temples. What strange permutations of people would she find swaying on the dance floor or tucked away in small corners? Nothing was quite as it had been, and she had the feeling that she was living by old rules while everyone else had adopted a new set without telling her.

She was, therefore, incapable of shock and surprise when she turned to find Reuben and Helen walking arm-in-arm out of the ballroom and looking into one another's eyes as if their glances had permanently locked into a mutual wavelength. Marybeth, Reuben, David, she murmured the names to herself, mentally counting fingers in her head, Betty . . . that leaves Marvin. She twisted around to see if she could find Marvin among the throng of faces, but he didn't seem to be in evidence, so she shrugged and made her way to the bar. The throbbing in her head had escalated to a far more painful pounding, and she had come to the conclusion that perhaps alcohol would dull the pain.

'Samantha darling!' The room whirled with her as she turned to face Josh. 'I've been looking all over for you.'

'Have you?' she asked.

His hand tucked under her elbow, his dark eyes smiled down at her. 'Didn't you think I would be?'

It was amazing what a white dinner jacket could do for a pair of broad shoulders and an already handsome face. Samantha's head took an extra, dizzying little spin and she swayed right into Josh's arms. 'I really wasn't worried,' she said as he pulled her to him.

His laugh was low. 'You shouldn't be.'

To her surprise—no, she shouldn't be surprised, should she? After all, the band was playing—she and Josh were now dancing together.

'Have I told you how beautiful you look tonight?'

The compliment insinuated itself between a memory of Josh walking out of the sea and a particularly bad throbbing over her left eye. And, instead of warming her, it triggered a suspicion that she had thought she had laid to rest days ago. *What a line*, a small internal voice said. *You think this guy is for real?*

She cleared her throat, looked up and discovered that she could drown in his eyes. 'N . . . no, you haven't.'

'Forgive me,' he said. 'You're very lovely.'

She swallowed. 'Thank you.'

'I've never really met anyone like you before.'

The oldest cliché in the book. You'd better face it, baby, this guy has to be getting paid to deliver dialogue like that.

Samantha tried to ignore her sly, inner voice and concentrate on what could be a delightful flirtation. 'Really?' she asked.

'Really. You're different, you know.'

'Oh—in what way?'

'Cranky, irritating, frustrating, maddening . . .'

'You sure know how to pay a compliment!'

' . . . interesting, sexy, exciting, fascinating.'

A particularly vicious throbbing at one temple almost made Samantha faint, but she tried to ignore that, too. 'Oh,' she said lightly, 'I'm sure you've met other sexy and fascinating women before.'

His voice was deep. 'None like you.'

Despite her headache, she was alert enough to ask the question that she hadn't managed to get to on the beach. 'Didn't you recently have a love affair that went bad?'

Josh paused for a moment and then once more swayed again with the music. 'How did you know about that?'

'Helen told me.'

'I see.'

'Well?'

He was silent, his eyes looking into the distance. Then he looked down at her once again. 'It was bad,' he said slowly, 'very bad.'

'What was she like?'

'Tall, dark-haired, attractive, very wealthy. She had more money than she knew what to do with.'

'That doesn't sound like a sin.'

'No, but it made her very vulnerable to boredom. You see, she had everything she wanted or, if she didn't have it, she could get it so easily that it lost all meaning for her. I'm afraid I wasn't quite in her financial league, and she eventually got weary of having to spend time with a man who had to work from nine to five.'

'So what happened?' she asked.

His mouth twisted into a wry slant. 'She went on to bigger and better things—a prince of something-or-other, I think.'

The pain he had suffered was so obvious that Samantha couldn't think of anything to say except, 'I'm sorry.'

He smiled down at her. 'You shouldn't be. I learned something from it.'

'What?'

'That I was tired of casual affairs that ended on sour notes, that I didn't want to be used any more, that I was looking for something more serious.'

Another agonising throb in her head made her look away from him and lean her cheek against his shoulder. But the pain wasn't enough to keep a note of triumph out of her inner dialogue. There, she said, is a man who has suffered and paid the price for it.

He wouldn't have lied about that.

Why not? It's a masterly way of eliciting sympathy.

And he's interested in me. You heard what he said—he's looking for something more serious. He likes me! He thinks I'm fascinating and lovely and sexy and. . .

The better to seduce you, my dear.

'Sam?' His head bent lower so that his lips were by her ear. 'You know I'm crazy about you, don't you?'

Anger, unhappiness and confusion mixed chaotically with the unmerciful pounding in her head. Nausea rose in her throat and pressed on the back of her tongue. The ballroom seemed to slip and spin about her, a multi-coloured cube turning on end, tumbling round and round until she had had to shut her eyes or she would begin to tumble, too.

'Sam? Are you feeling all right?'

But she had finally managed to extricate herself from his arms, pushing him away from her with the hardest shove she could manage and sending him sprawling into another couple. There were gasps and startled looks from those around them, but Samantha didn't stay long enough to apologise. She spun away, missing the expression of shock on his face and then the sudden anger, and ran as hard as she could, fighting furiously to keep her balance, to keep the room from heaving and throwing her to one side, to keep herself from knocking into anyone as she rushed out of the door and down the corridor.

Later, Samantha would have to give one of the stewards high marks for unflappability. He didn't seem at all surprised when she ran into him, a whirlwind of yellow silk, trembling dark curls and wide, frightened eyes, and asked him how she could make an emergency phone call to New York. 'From one of the hotels, miss.' Nor did he express shock when she demanded that the gangplank be put down again, saying that it was a matter of life and death. 'Of course,' he said soothingly and, after making her sit down in his small office, he phoned the ship's bridge. Within minutes, one of the ship's officers had arrived, had taken one look at Samantha's white face and agreed with the steward that there was probably just enough time left before embarking for Miss Lorimer to make her phone call.

The gangplank was lowered with due speed, and Samantha was escorted by the sympathetic officer off the boat, into a taxi and down to one of the hotels.

The hotel lobby's guests stared at her with fascination when she arrived, barefoot and clutching the officer's jacket over her shoulders. The hotel's telephone operator, a plump girl whose nonchalance was only matched by her boredom, shrugged and said, 'Sure, why not?' when the officer made his request. Then Samantha was put into the manager's deserted office where she could have some privacy, put the receiver of the phone to her ear and waited while the operator made the connection. After an interminable amount of time in which Samantha listened to assorted clickings and buzzings and tiredly imagined one tiny connector after another hooking together across thousands of miles, she finally heard a telephone ring. Despite the pounding in her skull which had grown to such proportions that it actually hurt to keep her head up straight, she stiffened in the chair.

'Hello,' a voice said.

Samantha felt a surge of relief. 'Grand. . . Margaret? It's Samantha.'

'This is Margaret Lorimer,' the voice said tinnily. 'Please don't be put off by this damned answering machine. I don't much like it either, but I've bowed to the demands of technology. I'm sorry I can't come to the phone right now, but Cassie and I decided that we couldn't stand New York one minute longer. So we're sunning ourselves in the Caribbean and will be back at the end of May. You can leave a message if you want after the machine beeps. 'Bye now.'

Samantha stared down at the receiver, winced when it beeped at her and then slowly put it back on its cradle, her shoulders slumping in helpless defeat. She'd never know now. Never. There was no way of proving or disproving the insinuations of that cruel inner voice.

In the nightmare that followed, she took a few steps to the door of the manager's office. The officer, who had been chatting up the receptionist, took one look at her and ran to her side. His horrified glance let Samantha know that she had finally started to look just as bad as she actually felt.

'Are you all right?' he asked.

Nausea caught hold of her and, swallowing convulsively, she shook her head.

'Can you get back to the boat?'

The words came out so low that he had to bend to hear them. 'I don't know.'

He took her arm. 'Take it easy now. One step at a. . .'

The door of the hotel was flung open, and Josh hurried in, the captain of the *Princess Marguerita* right behind him.

'Samantha! What's wrong?'

'Josh,' she said faintly.

He grabbed her, his hands strong, pulling her up to him. 'Sam, why did you run away?'

His face loomed over her. 'I. . .' But she could no longer speak. His dark eyes burned into her, piercing

her and then sucking her up into their depths. She
tried to swim against their strength and power; she
tried to fight their hold on her. She struggled and the
room began to sway around her, the faces of other
people disappearing into a mist of grey, noises fading
into a buzzing hum, light dimming until she could
barely see.

'I . . .' she started again, but it was too late. His
eyes seemed to grow so that they were no longer eyes
but pools, lakes, oceans. They sucked her in even further, swallowing her, pulling her under. Samantha
made one last effort to keep her head up, but she was
helpless against his force. The dark, dizzying waters
closed over her head, and she fainted, not knowing
that the whole room stood up in shock or that it was
Josh who picked her up, one arm under her knees,
the other under her shoulders so that her head lay
back against his arm. He gazed down at her with a
stricken look and then, pulling her up closer to him,
he buried his face in her neck.

The sun was a gold circle low in the velvety purple of
the southern sky, and balmy breezes caused the clear
blue water of the Caribbean to lap up against the
boat. It was the cocktail hour, and the waiter went
from lounge chair to lounge chair, taking drink
orders from passengers who were chatting or simply
lying back, letting the sun's rays heat their skin.
Down from the bar area were the ping-pong tables,
and the tiny slaps of small white balls against paddles
gave a rhythmic backdrop to the low murmurs of
conversation and the clink of glasses.

Margaret Lorimer was sitting on a lounge chair,
her tiny form wrapped in what appeared to be miles
of floating pink and white floral chiffon. She wore

glittering gold mules on her feet and had a delicate chain with a diamond 'M' wrapped around one small ankle. Her eyes were hidden by huge sunglasses and her white hair was twisted low on her neck into a chignon. In one beringed hand, she held a Martini, the other hand was gracefully gesturing in the air.

'No, darling,' she was saying to the blond and beautiful young man in the chaise-longue beside her, 'I'm simply not up to it. Shuffleboard takes up too much energy—all that bending and pushing! Besides, I've always been opposed to exercise. It's far too strenuous.'

To her left was Cassie on another chaise-longue. She provided a stark contrast to Margaret, being dressed in a sensible pale-grey dress and white shoes with foam treads. She wore a wide-brimmed straw coolie hat to keep the sun off her face, and she was alternately sipping at a lemonade and writing a letter. Cassie never went anywhere without her stationery box.

The sound of her pen on paper caused Margaret to glance over at her. 'Which one of your wretched relatives are you writing to now?'

'My niece.'

'Which one? You know I can never keep your hordes of relations straight.'

'The one in Akron.'

'The go-go dancer.'

'Ballroom dancer,' Cassie corrected her. 'She teaches ballroom dancing.'

'Hmph.' Margaret took a sip of her Martini. 'Teaching waltzes to a lot of old fogies!'

Cassie remained undisturbed. 'Foxtrots and cha-chas,' she said 'She's a good lass, and found herself a nice fellow, too.'

Margaret snorted once again, glanced at the blond young man at her side and said, 'Speaking of fellows, how do you suppose Samantha is getting on?'

'She'll be having a wonderful time, I'm sure.'

'That young lady has always been wound up tighter than a corkscrew. You know what her parents are like; Roger's so stuffy they could put him on a museum display. I don't know where he came from, I really don't. There isn't a bit of me in him.'

'He's a good provider.'

'Insurance!' Snort and another sip of Martini. 'Dull, dull, dull. And Diane isn't much better.'

'She's been a fine daughter-in-law to ye. When you were sick. . .'

Margaret sniffed. 'She disapproves of me, you know. Always has.'

'And I'm thinking that Samantha turned out just fine. She's a wee bit on the serious side, but there's no harm in that.'

'Serious? Samantha was ancient at five, and she isn't much better now. Well, I've done my best by her—a new hairdo, new clothes, sexy underwear to put her in the spirit of the thing. I just hope she can relax enough to enjoy it.'

'The lass is probably dancing her heart out with some lovely young man.'

Margaret perked up a bit. 'You think so? You think she'd know what to do with a lovely young man if she found him?'

'Well,' said Cassie, 'she's a Lorimer, isn't she?'

'Her father's a Lorimer, too, but if she's got one ounce of me in her. . . well, there's hope, then. Definitely hope.'

And with that statement, Margaret drained her Martini and, leaning back in her chair, closed her eyes and faced the sun.

CHAPTER ELEVEN

SAMANTHA opened her eyes and found herself staring once again at the blue curtains that covered the window of the ship's infirmary. They were patterned with tiny yellow roses, and the light coming in from behind the curtains turned the roses to a shimmering gold, a colour whose brightness caused Samantha to close her eyes hurriedly again. There was a refuge, she had already discovered, in the cool darkness behind her eyelids where sleep was capable of erasing pain and illness. It was a sanctuary that she had returned to time and again since that nightmarish evening of the telephone call and the hotel and her collapse into Josh's arms.

She had only the very faintest memory of what had actually happened that night. She could remember the tinny sound of her grandmother's recorded voice, the bright lights of the hotel lobby growing dark around her, Josh's white dinner jacket appearing to be a beacon in the growing mist. She could recall her yearning to reach him, the feel of his arms going around her, and then the frightening way their strength seemed to disappear when everything around her went black and she had slipped down into the void of oblivion.

What had happened after that, she knew only from the stories of other people. After her fainting spell, she had been rushed to a hospital where she was pronounced ill with a 'flu whose longevity and virulence

163

had already made it legendary in the Greek medical community. Since the 'flu was not wildly contagious or life-threatening, she had been brought back to the *Princess Marguerita* where she had been put to bed in the infirmary and tended by the ship's nurse, a large and severe woman, who had been looking after Samantha with a solicitude above and beyond the call of duty.

Not that Samantha had always been aware of what was going on. She had spent the first twenty-four hours semi-conscious and half delirious as the fever raged through her. Aspirin and alcohol rubs had brought the fever down to a manageable level and her nausea and dizziness had eventually disappeared, but the vicious headache had remained. This hyper-sensitivity and terrible head pain had lasted for two days, leaving in its wake a headache that she could just manage to tolerate and a weakness so pervasive that she barely had enough energy to get out of bed.

It was at this point in her illness that the captain of the ship had arrived to discuss the possibility that she might leave the ship at Crete, and Samantha had agreed that it was probably for the best. She hated the idea of staying in the infirmary for the next three days, but she couldn't imagine how she would cope with the landing in Athens. It was hard enough to get around a foreign city when one was in the best of health; it seemed insurmountable to her when she was in pain and as weak as a kitten. So she had no choice but to acquiesce when he had told her that the ship had been in communication with a travel agent on Crete, who had confirmed a reservation in her name for an Olympic Airlines flight from Crete to Athens and a TWA flight from Athens to New York.

The news that Samantha was about to leave the ship in mid-cruise and was well enough to receive visitors had brought friends and acquaintances down to the infirmary for bedside chats.

Marybeth had walked into Samantha's small room in the infirmary with a bouncy step and a wide smile. She'd looked like health personified, blonde and tanned, the golden shade of her skin contrasting with the white of her tennis clothes. When she had seen Samantha flat on her back, her eyes sunken and her face pale, she had tried to douse the happy expression and appear duly sorrowful and sympathethic, but the smile kept breaking through her attempt at solemnity the way the sun insists upon breaking through a thin layer of cloud.

'What's the good news?' Samantha had asked.

Marybeth sat down on the chair, took one of Samantha's hands and ignored her question. 'Honeychile, you had us all so worried! Why, you've got no idea how frightened we were. We've been checking our temperatures and looking out for spots and. . .'

'Spots?'

'As in measles and chickenpox and scarlet fever.'

Samantha couldn't help laughing even though doing so made her head ache. 'I've only got 'flu! Come on, Marybeth, what's been happening? I saw some odd things at the dance the night I got sick.'

'Odd things? What odd things?'

Marybeth was fingering the pleats on her short white tennis skirt, but Samantha wasn't deceived either by her seeming nonchalance or her seeming ignorance. 'Things between you and David, Reuben and Helen, Betty and the purser.'

'Well,' said Marybeth, 'Betty has had a thing going with the purser since before Rhodes. He's unmarried and crazy about her.'

'And Reuben?'

Marybeth shrugged. 'He likes glamorous widows. He and the redhead have been inseparable for days.'

'And how does David fit into all this?'

Marybeth had the decency to look a bit shamefaced. 'Now, Samantha, I know this is going to sound just awful, but David and I had concocted. . . well, a scheme to make you and Reuben jealous.'

'Jealous?'

'Well, neither of us were getting anywhere, you see, so I suggested to David that he and I act as if we were madly keen on one another. That way you two would feel threatened and realise just how much you liked us.' She cleared her throat. 'Am I making sense?'

'I'm afraid so,' Samantha said drily.

'Now, honeybunch, don't go all moral on me. Everything's fair in the war between the sexes—that's how I look on it. But the trouble was. . . well, that David and I. . .' and she blushed a fiery red, 'well, we discovered that we liked each other instead.' She leaned forward. 'You really don't care, do you?'

Samantha shook her head. 'I've never been interested in David in that way. You've known that.'

Marybeth sat back and let out a sigh of relief. 'Well, I thought that was the case, but I did just have a niggling worry that you might have been playing a very deep game with him.'

Samantha gave her a weary smile. 'I'm not capable of deep games.'

'I've tired you out,' Marybeth said guiltily. 'I'd better go before that dragon of a nurse out there attacks me.' She stood up and smoothed down her tennis skirt.

'Marybeth——?' Samantha began.

'Yes?'

'Is. . . has. . . I just wondered if. . .'

Marybeth gave her a knowing smile. 'If it's Josh you're worried about, you shouldn't be. He and the dragon have practically come to blows.'

'Oh.' Samantha could feel her cheeks redden.

'Just tell me one thing, honeychile. How on earth did you manage to steal him away from the rapacious redhead? I tried everything in my repertoire, but it didn't work. I could have sworn that you didn't even lift your little finger, and he came running. And when I remember how you two didn't get along at first. . .' She shook her head in admiration. 'Just tell me how you did it.'

Samantha wished she had the answer to that question, but she hadn't a clue. She'd never known why Josh had, all of a sudden, taken such an interest in her. And it was that uncertainty that had led her into such ridiculous suspicions as believing that he had been hired by Fantasy Unlimited to sweep her off her feet. Of course, she now understood that her paranoia had been the result of the 'flu.

'I don't know how I did it,' she said weakly. 'I guess it was my scintillating conversation.'

'You are a very intelligent person,' Marybeth agreed.

'Men don't fall for intelligence,' Samantha replied wryly and from long experience. 'They only respect it.'

'Well,' said Marybeth, 'you must have what it takes. Goodness knows how you did, Samantha, but you've managed the impossible.'

'The impossible?'

'Hooking the handsomest and most eligible man on the *Princess Marguerita*,' Marybeth said with conviction. 'And he's smitten, honeybunch. Absolutely smitten!'

The handsomest and most eligible man on the *Princess Marguerita* wasn't actually thinking about the state of his heart at the moment. He was having another irritating conversation with the nurse who had guarded Samantha's door with such a vengeance that he'd been ready to throttle her any number of times in the past few days. In fact, he had got so frustrated with her that he'd actually had dreams about her. In one of them, her grey corkscrew curls turned into snakes and her heavy features into the face of a stubborn mule.

'I'm sorry,' she was saying smugly, 'but you can't go in until the other visitor leaves. I'm afraid Miss Lorimer doesn't have the strength to cope with more than one person at a time.'

'I'd like to know how she copes with you,' Josh muttered impatiently through clenched teeth as he leaned against the door-jamb of the infirmary.

The nurse, who had been studying a file in front of her, now looked up at him through her steel-rimmed glasses and said frostily, 'I beg your pardon?'

'Nothing,' he said, and clutched the bouquet of roses he had brought so tightly that a thorn broke the skin on his thumb. He cursed under his breath and was sucking his finger when the door to Samantha's room opened and Marybeth came bouncing out.

'Next,' she said gaily, giving Josh a saucy grin.

'Just a minute,' said the nurse, standing up. 'I'll have to check and see if Miss Lorimer can handle another visitor.'

Marybeth took one look at Josh's face as the nurse disappeared into Samantha's room and laughed. 'She's a dragon, isn't she?'

'A gorgon,' he said. 'How's Samantha?'

'Tired, I think. She's awfully pale.'

'I. . .'

'I'm sorry,' the nurse said, reappearing in the doorway, 'but I believe Miss Lorimer is in no condition. . .'

Josh glared at her. 'Did you tell her who I was?'

The nurse's lips pressed together. 'I don't see that it matters who you are.'

'This is it,' he muttered to Marybeth. 'I've had it!' And before Marybeth's delighted eyes, he advanced on the nurse, brandishing his bouquet of roses. 'Move!' he demanded.

'If you think. . .'

'Move!'

It was obvious that the nurse had never before seen a bouquet of roses wielded as if it were a weapon, but she took one look at the waving flowers and then at Josh's determined face and had enough sense to know that discretion is the better part of valour.

She moved one step to the side and gave him a slit-eyed look. 'If you're not out of there in five minutes,' she said threateningly, 'then. . .'

'Then what?' he countered with equal menace.

'Then I'll call the captain.'

But by that time Josh wouldn't have even cared if he'd been told he had to walk the plank. He had entered the bedroom and seen Samantha lying there, pale and fragile against the white of the sheets, her eyes dark smudges in her face, her hair a tangle of curls on the pillow. She wore a white nightgown with blue ribbons threaded through eyelets at the neck, and at the sight of her, his heart twisted, tightened, made his breath come short.

'Sam?' he said, closing the door behind him.

'Were you and the nurse having a battle?' she asked, her smile wan.

'I won,' he said, putting the flowers on the table beside her bed and then sitting down in the chair. 'How are you?' he added.

'Recovering.'

He took one of her hands in his. The skin was cool, but her hand felt incredibly delicate as if she'd lost a lot of weight. He could feel each separate bone and tendon.

'You have to be careful,' he told her. 'The doctors said that if you don't give yourself a chance to get well, you could get complications.'

'I know,' Samantha said. 'I'm being a superlative patient.'

She smiled again and pulled herself upright against the pillows, but Josh could see how much the effort cost her. She went even paler if that were possible, and the hand he was holding trembled slightly. He had an overwhelming urge to take her in his arms, but he was also afraid he might crush her. She seemed so thin, so pale, so ethereal.

'Are you eating anything?' he asked in concern.

In spite of her frailty, Samantha's sense of humour had not deserted her. 'Well, Dr Sinclair, I'm about to graduate from chicken soup to beef broth. It's supposed to be very invigorating and build up the blood and all that sort of thing.'

Josh was quite willing to fall into the spirit of the thing. He would have done anything at this point to make Samantha happy. 'And how about your temperature, Miss Lorimer? Has it been normal?'

'I think so.'

He put a clinical hand to her forehead. 'Cool,' he pronounced. 'You just might make it.'

'What a relief!'

'And your pulse.' He pressed a finger to her wrist. 'A bit rapid. Is there any reason for that?'

Her face was solemn. 'Not that I know of, doctor.'

'Of course, I'm worried about those heart palpitations.'

Samantha gave him an uneasy look. 'What heart palpitations?'

'They're very typical of 'flu.'

'I haven't had any heart palpitations.'

'You're sure?'

'I. . .'

But Josh had leaned forward and placed a hand below her left breast. Through the thin fabric of her nightgown he could feel the warmth and wonderful weight of her, the steady trip-trip of her heart. 'No heart palpitations,' he said jokingly, but when he looked up at her, he saw tears in her eyes and nothing could stop him from moving over to the bed, taking her in his arms, crushing her towards him, holding her so close that both of them could hardly breathe.

'Sam,' he said into the soft skin of her neck where the silky curls began. 'Please don't cry. I didn't mean to hurt you.'

Her voice wavered. 'You didn't hurt me.'

'Then why. . .?' He loosened his hold and looked down at her.

Her eyelashes were damp and spiky; tears turned her eyes to a brilliant blue. 'Josh, I shouldn't have run away from you like that. It was so foolish and dumb. You can't imagine what I'd been thinking, and. . .'

'Hush!' He could feel her distress in the trembling of her body, and he held her even closer, his hand stroking her curls. He had so many things to tell her, so many actions to explain. 'Listen, Sam, I'm the one who's been the idiot.'

'No, I've. . .'

There was a knock at the door. 'Mr Sinclair? Your time is up.'

'God damn that nurse! When are you leaving?'

'This afternoon—at about four o'clock.'

'Are you strong enough for the trip?'

'The entire airline has been alerted,' Samantha said wryly. 'I'll have a wheelchair at every airport and stewardesses hovering over me.'

'Sam. . .'

'Mr Sinclair! Your time is up!'

'God!' There was no time to tell her everything in his heart. He couldn't even explain how he had tried unsuccessfully to get a seat on her flights so that he could accompany her back to New York. He couldn't begin to sort through the complexities of his emotions for her, the changes he'd been through, the knowledge that had come to him when she had collapsed in his arms. 'Sam,' he said hurriedly, 'we have to talk.'

'But. . .'

'I'm going to try to get back to New York as soon as I can. I've got your address from the purser and I'll come and see you.'

'Oh, Josh!' She was so weak that the slightest emotion made her cry, and the tears started again, brimming in her eyes and tumbling down her pale cheeks.

Josh touched a salty drop with his finger. 'I. . .'

The door was flung open, and the nurse stood in it, her arms akimbo, elbows jutting out, her hands planted on her wide hips. She took in the sight of Josh with a tearful Samantha in his arms and said coldly, 'I knew you were going to upset my patient. Kindly get off that bed.'

Josh ignored her. 'Sam, I . . .'

'Off!'

The nurse was bearing down on them, an outraged tank of a woman, ready to do battle wherever necessary. He took one quick glance at her, gave Samantha one final tight hug and finally said what he'd been trying to say ever since his arrival into that tiny room. He didn't want the nurse to hear, so he dropped his voice to its lowest register and whispered the words very lightly into the ivory shell of Samantha's ear.

'I love you,' he said.

Samantha hummed happily to herself as she walked up to her grandmother's apartment building. There were a number of reasons why she felt so happy. First of all, Manhattan's uncertain weather had turned quite definitely into spring on this lovely Sunday afternoon. The sun was shining, the air was balmy and the sounds of birds singing could be heard even over the ever-present drone of city traffic. Then there was the state of her health. Four days had passed since her return from Greece, and she was once again feeling like her normal self. The headache had finally disappeared and, with it, the awful weakness that had made her tremble and flush and cry at every little thing that happened to her. This morning she had got up, finally unpacked her suitcases, energetically cleaned her apartment and, in looking at a mirror, had discovered that, apart from an excessive thinness, the old Samantha was back.

But the best thing of all was that she was now well enough to take pleasure in her last memories of the cruise. She'd been ill, it was true, but she could, with perfect recall, remember Josh's arms around her, his concern for her and the words he had whispered in her ear. He loved her, he had said so. She had thought such a thing impossible; over and over again, she had reminded herself that what had happened on the cruise was artificial, unreal, a stage set where emotions were exaggerated and blown out of proportion. The cruise had seemed like one enormous illusion. Look at the way everyone had changed partners halfway through as if they'd been part of a large board game where luck, a dice throw, the spin of a wheel could alter emotions, feelings, attractions.

But Josh's words had rung true. There had been sincerity in them, intense feeling and a desperation that she recognised as akin to her own. In the midst of all that falseness, he had, as she had, not been able to trust his own emotions. It had taken her a long while to understand that she had fallen in love with Josh; she could understand why it had taken him even longer to realise that he had fallen in love with her. *Fallen in love with her*. Samantha hugged the words to herself, cherished them, luxuriated in them and, in doing so, discovered that they had changed the world for her. The sky seemed that much bluer, the air that much sweeter, the sun that much brighter.

'Hello, Miss Lorimer. You're looking chipper today.'

'Thank you, Thomas, you're looking pretty good yourself.'

'Oh, I'm getting a little creaky around the knees, but I get around.'

Samantha smiled at him as he gave her the keys to her grandmother's apartment. Thomas must be close to seventy years old, an elderly gentleman who had a full head of white hair and who wore his uniform with as much spit and polish as a five-star general. He had acted as both building superintendent and weekend doorman for as long as Samantha could remember.

'Your grandmother is sure keen on telegrams. I thought the end of the world had come last night when I got mine,' he told her.

Samantha knew what Thomas meant. Most people used telegrams for emergencies, but Margaret used them for personal letters. This time the one sent to Samantha had been particularly imperious. She was ordered to 'Go to the apartment and make head or tail out of the mail. Stop. Thomas will give you the key. Stop.' No pleases, no thank yous, no explanations. Just typical Margaret!

'Do you know when she's coming back, Thomas?'

'I'm afraid not, Miss Lorimer. She isn't the type to stick to a schedule anyway. But we do know one thing.'

'What's that?'

'Whatever she's doing she's having a whale of a time!'

Samantha was still smiling when the elevator ponderously and creakily arrived at the fifth floor. The building was elegant but also old, and the lock on the door to her grandmother's apartment complained as she twisted the key in it. Inside the apartment, the air was cool but slightly stale, and the furniture sat in the darkness. Samantha opened the curtain in the den to let in some light, then sneezed when a small tornado of dust was raised by the swinging fabric.

The den was one of the smallest rooms in the apartment, a cubbyhole, really, with an ornately carved wooden desk in it, a chair and a small book-case. On the desk was a huge pile of envelopes of all kinds and sizes.

Sitting down, Samantha began to separate the mail; Cassie's to one side and Margaret's in two piles, business and personal. She knew why the telegram had come: Margaret wanted Samantha to pay her bills. She had a horror of being charged interest just because she was on vacation and couldn't pay her charge accounts on time. Samantha sorted the envel-opes quickly. Bloomingdale's. Saks Fifth Avenue. American Express. Bendel's, Alexander's. Fortu-noff's. Fantasy Unlimited. Gristede's. *Fantasy Unlimited!*

Samantha stared at the envelope and then smiled to herself. It was probably just part of the corre-spondence that had been required to cancel the fantasy her grandmother had purchased for her. Dear, sweet Margaret, who had been convinced that her granddaughter was totally incapable of finding a man on her own. As she opened the envelope, Samantha contemplated with a happy serenity just how surprised Margaret was going to be when she discovered that her granddaughter was not only fully capable of finding a wonderful, sexy man, but also of falling in love with him and having that love whole-heartedly returned. She imagined with great pleasure Margaret's shocked expression and Cassie's surprise and approval. She had those faces in her mind's eye when she removed the letter from the envelope and unfolded it.

In compliance with your own private fantasy, she read, *a shipboard romance in the Greek Islands. Paid in full.*

The last three words had been handwritten, in blue ink, in a rounded script.

Paid in full.

Samantha stared at the letter and then said with a disbelieving voice as she pushed back her chair, 'Oh, no. Absolutely not. Never!'

Why keep deluding yourself, baby? Here it is—the truth, the whole truth and nothing but the truth.

Samantha would have dearly loved to know where the voice came from, that way she could slam the door on it for ever. She hated its cruel cynicism and ugly turn of phrase. She had no reason, she told herself firmly, to doubt Josh or the fact that he loved her. She had no reason, she reassured herself, to believe that he had been contracted to speak those words to her, to have been paid several thousands of dollars to perform. . .

Sex acts, love acts. Words of sweet nothing spoken into your ear.

Samantha's jaw clenched with an audible crack and, although it was Sunday, she pulled the telephone to her, scattering bills and letters in every direction. With fingers that were cold but steady, she picked up the receiver and dialled. Somewhere in Manhattan, in an office building perhaps, a phone rang and rang and rang. She could imagine it there, the sound echoing from the walls, the ceiling and the floor. She could picture the empty desk, the covered typewriter, the tidy in-basket, pens and pencils neatly arranged in the top drawer. Finally, when it was quite obvious that the Bell system had done the best for her that it could, she slammed down the receiver.

Good try, sweetheart, but let's just face the facts, shall we?

She knew the facts, she told herself and, carefully folding the Fantasy Unlimited invoice in half, she put it in her bag.

He was playing with you, having a good time. There are lots of men like that—tomcats who sniff after every available . . .

With a superhuman effort of will-power, she stifled the voice, pushed it far down to the bottom of her mind and ignored its clamouring attempts to rise the surface once again. And then, with the sort of calm that is born out of sheer desperation, she rearranged the scattered envelopes and began to open Margaret's bills, one by one.

The buzzing came out of a dark haze. At first it came in spurts, but then it seemed to swoop down on her and then flit around her head like a heavy, droning bee. Restlessly, Samantha turned over, but the buzzing continued, an incessant and irritating sound. Finally she opened her eyes, stared into the darkness and realised that it was the sound of the buzzer on her intercom, the one that connected the outer lobby of her building to her apartment.

She reached up, switched on the light on her bedside-table and wearily glanced at her watch. Four in the morning. Who, in God's name. . .? *Josh.* No, it couldn't be. The cruise would just be over; he would barely have had time. . . but the thought that it might be Josh at her door electrified her and, pushing off the marmalade cat that slept on her feet, she jumped out of bed and ran into the hallway, groping down its darkness until she felt the button to her intercom. She leaned on it hard.

'Yes?'

'Sam?'

His voice was tinny and distorted by the speaker, but she couldn't help the leap of her heart. 'Josh, it's four o'clock!'

'I know, but the plane was late. Can I come up?'

'Hold on. I'll buzz the door open.'

As soon as she'd done that, Samantha raced back to the bathroom, where she dragged on the blue terry bathrobe that hung on the door's hook and then ran a comb through her unruly curls, scrubbed her face and brushed her teeth. Then, when the doorbell rang, she raced back down the hallway, spent what seemed like forever trying to unlock all the hooks and chains on the door with shaking fingers, and finally flung the door open, to find Josh standing there, looking as if he'd just been through a war, His suit was rumpled, his hair fell forward on to his forehead, there were dark circles under his eyes and he was badly in need of a shave.

For a few seconds they just stared at one another, Josh leaning against his suitcases, Samantha breathing as if she'd just run a marathon.

Then she said, 'I guess you'd better come in before we wake the neighbours.'

And he said, 'That sounds like a good idea.'

She cleared her throat. 'You can put your suitcases here in the hall.'

Josh heaved the first of his suitcases into the foyer. 'You're recovered from the 'flu?'

'Oh, yes, I feel fine.'

The second suitcase followed. 'That's good.'

The door closed behind him and suddenly her foyer seemed smaller and narrower than it had ever been. Josh loosened his tie with his forefinger, and Samantha said nervously, 'You could hang your jacket in the closet.'

His dark eyes were grave as they studied her flushed face. 'Thanks.'

'And. . . er. . . would you like some coffee?'

'That would be nice.'

'Milk? Sugar?'

'Just black, please.'

As he was taking off his jacket, Samantha fled down the hallway to the kitchen. Her heart was pounding and her hands were still trembling as she filled the coffee percolator with water and put mugs and spoons on the counter. Not even the homey, safe warmth of her kitchen or the comforting sensation of Ginger, her marmalade cat, winding through her legs made her relax. He's a stranger, she was thinking with despair. A handsome stranger that she'd met on a vacation, and she hadn't a clue who he was or what he might. . .

'You have a nice place,' said Josh, and Samantha whirled around to find that he was standing in the doorway, carefully watching her.

The sugar bowl clattered as she put it down by the sink. 'Thanks. I. . . like it a lot.' And then, because she was afraid of the awkward silence that might ensue, Samantha added in a bright and brittle voice that made her inwardly wince, 'Was your flight hard?'

'Twenty-two hours with an hour and a half delay in Rome.'

'That must have been exhausting.'

'It was.'

'You must be tired.'

'Very.'

This time there was a silence, and it was just as awful and as awkward as Samantha had feared. To fill it up, she hurriedly opened a drawer and pulled out some napkins.

Josh stepped forward. 'For God's sake. . .' he began, and then tripped, falling over Ginger, who had left the safety of Samantha's legs to investigate those of the stranger and begun to make sinuous S's around his ankles.

'I'm sorry,' Samantha said hurriedly, picking up Ginger and holding the cat's warm, furry body close to her chest as if it were a protective shield. 'It's just my cat.'

Josh straightened up. 'I noticed that,' he said grimly.

'She likes strangers.'

'Does she?'

'Yes, and she's very. . .'

'All right, Sam,' he said, and she could see the muscles in his jaw twitch as he clenched his teeth. 'If it's all over. If it was just a game you were playing and now it's over, for God's sake just say so. I've been through that sort of thing before, and I have no intention of being dragged through the wringer again. Not by you or anyone else.'

Samantha stared at him. 'What?'

'I know what these cruises are like,' Josh went on. 'There's a lot of fooling around, a lot of infatuations that die a quick death when it's over. People go home and suddenly remember that they've got a boyfriend in the wings or that they never really liked brown eyes in the first place.'

He would have gone on, but Samantha stopped him. 'You think I was playing around with you?' she asked incredulously.

'Just tell the truth,' he said coldly. 'That's all I want.'

'Well, that's what I want, too,' she said hotly. 'And I'd like to know all about your connection with Fantasy Unlimited.'

'Fantasy—what?'

Samantha had dropped Ginger to the floor and grabbed her bag which was sitting on the counter. She opened it and pulled out the Fantasy Unlimited invoice. 'Explain this,' she said, waving the paper at him.

Josh took it from her, read it and then glanced up. 'What the hell is it?'

She raised her chin. 'A gift from my grandmother—along with the cruise. It's a paid. . . fantasy, a romance. I didn't want it; I told her I didn't and I thought she'd cancelled it. But, as you can see, she didn't.'

'A paid romance? You mean this company would pay some man to give you a romance?'

'Yes.'

'With all the trimmings?'

There was a small glitter of amusement in his eyes that made her even angrier. 'I didn't enquire into the details,' she said coldly. 'I didn't want it.'

His amusement was spreading. It had gone from lighting his eyes to turning his mouth up into a grin. 'Now, let me get this straight. You think I was involved in this. You think that I was hired by this. . . Fantasy Unlimited to give you a shipboard romance.'

Samantha wasn't going to let him laugh at her. 'Weren't you?' she flung at him.

'Sam, are crazy?'

'I'm not crazy,' she said angrily. 'I just wondered about the dancing and kisses under the moonlight, the single rose on my bed, and all the sexy innuendoes.'

Josh stared at her for a second and then said, 'All right, I'll confess—I wanted to sweep you off your feet so high that you wouldn't know when you'd landed. It had nothing to do with a paid fantasy, but it was done in cold blood.' He gave a short, rueful laugh. 'I guess I wasn't very good at it, actually—a grade B lover!'

On the contrary, he'd been so marvellous at it that Samantha had fallen hook, line and sinker, but she wasn't about to tell him that. 'So you *were* manipulating me,' she said, then spat out the words, 'You might as well have been paid!' And, turning away from him so that he couldn't see the hurt on her face, she put her hands on the counter and clenched its sharp edge hard, not hearing as Josh crushed the Fantasy Unlimited invoice into a ball and threw it on the floor.

'Sam,' he said gently, coming up behind her and putting his hands on her shoulders, 'it was a lot nastier than that. You see, I'd been jilted badly, and I was pretty bitter about it. I had the feeling that all women were rotten, not just the one I'd fallen for. I couldn't strike back at her, but I wanted revenge. Unfortunately, you were my first victim.' The hands were softly kneading her shoulders, and Samantha stared, unseeing, at the textured, grainy wood of her cabinets. 'I didn't pick you out deliberately,' he went on. 'And I can't even say that what I did was done consciously. It was just that I couldn't keep you out of my mind despite all the fighting and arguments over the room. And then, after the night of the storm, I heard Marybeth telling that boyfriend of yours that you couldn't stand me. I told myself that it was a challenge, and I was going to prove to myself, to you and everyone else on that damn boat, that, on the contrary, you were so attracted to me that I could get you into bed any time I wanted.'

It was hard to let him see just how much his words cut into her, but Samantha turned around to face him. 'And did you prove it to yourself?' she asked. 'Are you happy now?'

'Sam.' His hands cupped her face, his thumbs stroked her cheeks. 'I fell in love with you. In the middle of it all, I fell head over heels in love with you. You were funny and interesting and unpredictable and. . .Sam, I didn't know it until you fainted in my arms, but when I took one look at your face, I suddenly realised. . . Sam, you believe me, don't you?' His eyes gazed deeply into hers and then he added with an obvious wrench, 'If you want me to leave, it you want me to walk out of your life, I'll understand.'

Samantha looked into the depths of his eyes and saw the misery there and the load of guilt he'd been carrying, and the small ray of hope. It came to her then that the cruise was finally over and, with it, all the deceptions and dishonesty, the illusions and false drama, that fantasy had woven into its enticing, sticky web. And what was left now that the façade had been stripped away was the truth: the plain, unvarnished and wonderful truth.

His hands dropped down to his sides. 'Tell me to get out, Sam,' he said slowly. 'Go ahead—I'll deserve it.'

Happiness had begun to grow inside her like a small kernel of sunshine. It spread, its rays reaching into every part of her being and raising her temperature to a delightful, tingling warmth. But she didn't let him see it. Coldly, she said, 'I want to know one thing.'

'What?' he asked warily.

'How you knew all that stuff about the bra I was wearing.'

He blinked. 'The bra?'

'When I was sleeping—that first time we met.'

'Oh, that.' He had the grace to look ashamed. 'Well, you see I had a girlfriend once who left the exact same model in my apartment after she moved out. Er—I should have thrown it out, but I never. . . er. . . seemed to get around to it.'

'You mean—you kept it like a trophy?'

Josh cleared his throat. 'It's better than putting notches in the headboard of my bed, don't you think?'

'What I think,' she said severely, 'is that your trophy days are over.'

'My trophy days. . .' he began. The wary look on his face had disappeared and that sexy, lazy, attractive grin had come back. 'Are you trying to tell me something, Sam?'

'You'll have to guess,' she said.

'You're not letting me off lightly, are you?'

'Uh-uh,' she said, shaking her head firmly. 'You don't deserve it.'

'Right,' said Josh, then took a deep breath. 'I have fallen hopelessly in love with you, Miss 93rd Street, and want to suggest that, if you reciprocate my feelings, we might like to commemorate the occasion by deciding on co-habitation leading to the marital state.'

Samantha was enjoying herself too much to let him off so easily. Her blue eyes danced as she said in a musing tone, 'I suppose I could take it under consideration.'

But she had just managed to push Josh beyond the limits of his patience. 'The hell with this,' he muttered to no one in particular and, pulling her roughly into his arms, he bent his dark head over hers and gave her the sort of full, hot and passionate kiss that a woman dreams about in her deepest fantasies. Closing her eyes, Samantha allowed herself to revel in all the sensations that came with it; the heat of his tongue, the softness of his lips, the slight roughness of his skin where his beard was coming in.

'Mmm,' she said when it was over. 'That was nice.'

Josh lifted her chin with his finger. 'You liked that, did you?' he asked softly.

'Uh-uh.'

'There's more where that came from.'

'I know,' she whispered.'

'Sam. . .?'

She didn't have the heart to tease him any longer. There was a question in his eyes that had to be answered, a need that had to be filled, a desire that had to be satiated. 'I love you,' she said softly.

His lips moved as if he couldn't speak and then he said in a low voice, 'Do you?'

'Oh, yes,' she said firmly, 'I do.' And, as she took him by the hand and led him to her bedroom, she fully intended to show him just how much.

Their wedding was small and simple, a ceremony at a church near their new apartment and a buffet reception afterwards. The guests totalled about fifty, including Josh's and Samantha's business partners, his parents and hers, assorted friends and relatives. Josh wore a dark blue business suit, and Samantha a long white gown with a veil that had given her the sensation of floating in a misty space as she had walked up the aisle. For her bridal bouquet, she carried roses, which wasn't exactly traditional, but had afforded both of them the kind of amusement that comes when two people share a small and very private joke.

Near the end of the reception, Margaret took Samantha aside.

'Well,' she said, 'I never thought I'd see the day you'd be married.'

'Was I that bad?' Samantha asked, and smiled as she looked down at her diminutive grandmother. In honour of this wedding, Margaret had outdone herself. She was wearing a gold lamé turban, a matching long gown with rhinestones on the high collar and cuffs, and glittering gold shoes. Her face was so made up that even her wrinkles glowed and, when she batted her eyes at anyone, the fake lashes trembled.

'Almost hopeless,' Margaret said. 'It took some doing to get you into shape.'

Samantha didn't mind that Margaret insisted on taking the credit for her wedding. 'Josh is nice, isn't he?' she asked.

'Hmph,' Margaret said. 'What's quite clear to me is that, finally, you've got a man who knows how to act in bed.'

Samantha enacted mock-shock. 'Grandmother!'

But Margaret ignored her. She tapped Samantha's hand with an imperious finger. 'And the way to keep him is to stay mysterious and seductive and alluring. Take it from me, my dear, I've had three husbands, and I know what I'm talking about.'

Samantha didn't doubt it for a minute, but there was one thing she'd been waiting to ask her grandmother and had been saving it for such an opportunity as this one. 'Margaret, why did you pay Fantasy Unlimited, when you'd cancelled my Greek romance?'

Margaret had taken a cigarette out of her jewelled case and was now inserting it in a jewelled cigarette holder. 'Why?' she asked. 'My dear, I don't see any point in wasting a perfectly good fantasy.'

'But who on earth. . .?' Samantha stared at her grandmother who was casually lighting her cigarette. 'Oh, Margaret, you didn't!'

'Certainly I did,' Margaret said calmly. 'My Caribbean cruise would have been an utter bore otherwise.'

And Samantha started to laugh. Laughter bubbled and welled out of her, and it was so infectious that even Margaret laughed and, when Josh looked in her direction, he too smiled and then lifted his glass to her as if he were making a toast. *I love you*. Silently, he mouthed the words to her.

I love you, too. She mouthed the words back. *Very, very much.*

Harlequin Presents

Coming Next Month

1023 TOO SHORT A BLESSING Penny Jordan
After the tragic death of her fiancé, a young Englishwoman becomes convinced that she'll never fall in love again—until she meets a very determined man who has every intention of changing her mind...and reaching her heart.

1024 MASQUERADE MARRIAGE Flora Kidd
On a Caribbean cruise, Carlotta discovers that the deckhand paying so much attention to her is really a bodyguard hired by her wealthy father because of kidnapping threats. The complication of their falling in love is not part of the plan.

1025 CIRCLE OF FATE Charlotte Lamb
Things get complicated when Melanie, already doubtful about her engagement to a prominent businessman, meets another man who infuriates her, but also attracts her. Breaking off her engagement, however, doesn't immediately bring about the desired results!

1026 A RACY AFFAIR Roberta Leigh
Emma Fielding, governess to a racing car driver's motherless child, is persuaded to marry him so there'll be a guardian in case of his death. When they fall in love with each other, they're too afraid at first to admit it.

1027 OUT OF THE SHADOWS Sandra Marton
When Lauren meets the man she knows is right for her, past bitterness between their families threatens their love. Can they selfishly ignore the hurtful consequences of their actions to achieve a happy future together?

1028 BRITTANY'S CASTLE Leigh Michaels
Successful banker Brittany Masters reluctantly agrees to a mock reconciliation with her unfaithful husband until he obtains a government appointment. In return he'll give her a divorce. The situation is awkward, but happily nothing turns out as they expect.

1029 NO STRINGS ATTACHED Annabel Murray
When lively, actively social, travel agent Vita, believing in love and commitment, meets attractive but footloose Dominic, looking for a temporary affair, conflict is inevitable. So, too, is love—but in between is a time of turmoil.

1030 TOUCH AND GO Elizabeth Oldfield
That it turns out to be a hoax, doesn't make her stepfather's kidnapping any less harrowing for Karis, visiting him in Bangkok. Especially when the only one she can turn to is the man she'd loved and broken off with six months before.

Available in November wherever paperback books are sold, or through Harlequin Reader Service:

In the U.S.
901 Fuhrmann Blvd.
P.O. Box 1397
Buffalo, N.Y. 14240-1397

In Canada
P.O. Box 603
Fort Erie, Ontario
L2A 5X3

Can you keep a secret?

You can keep this one plus 4 free novels

Harlequin Intrigue
Adopts a New Cover Story!

We are proud to present to you
the new Harlequin Intrigue cover design.

Look for these exciting new stories, which mix a contemporary, sophisticated romance with the surprising twists and turns of a puzzler . . . romance with "something more."

Plus . . . we are also offering you the chance to enter the Intrigue Mystery Weekend Sweepstakes in the October Intrigue titles. Win one of four mysterious and romantic weekends.

Buy the October Harlequin Intrigues!

INTNC